A Horse Called Saskatoon

JoAnne Chitwood Nowack

Sequel to *A Horse Called Tamarindo*

REVIEW AND HERALD® PUBLISHING ASSOCIATION
HAGERSTOWN, MD 21740

The author assumes full responsibility for the accuracy
of all facts and quotations as cited in this book.

Texts credited to Clear Word are from *The Clear Word,*
copyright © 1994 by Jack J. Blanco.

This book was
Edited by Andy Nash
Cover designed by Willie Duke
Cover illustration by Scott Snow
Electronic makeup by Shirley M. Bolivar
Typeset: 12.5/14 Times New Roman

PRINTED IN U.S.A.

05 04 03 02 01   5 4 3 2 1

R&H Cataloging Service
Nowack, JoAnne Chitwood
    A horse called Saskatoon.

    I. Title.

813.6

ISBN 0-8280-1562-7

DEDICATION

To my husband, David,
with deep love and gratitude
for having such a best friend
with whom to share life's adventures.

CHAPTER ONE

Tory adjusted her wedding veil and peered through the netting, straining to see if she could spot Adam in one of the many cars making their way slowly up the winding drive to the sprawling ranch house where she waited. She caught her breath once again as she gazed out over the rolling Oregon hills below. Vast stands of Douglas fir, western larch, and hemlock trees stood like sentinels guarding the borders of lush vineyards.

"It's beautiful, isn't it, Robyn?" She sighed and turned to take a huge bouquet of white daisies from her best friend. "How perfect to have the wedding here at Adam's folks' place. It's like something from a fairy tale."

Robyn nodded, tears welling up in her dark eyes. "I'm really happy for you, Tory Butler," she said softly. "Everything *is* perfect. You and Adam together after everything you went through in Honduras . . ."

Her voice trailed off as she gazed out the window. Then her eyes opened wide in excitement. "They're here!" she shrieked. "The horses are here!"

A shiny black coach pulled by two mammoth Belgian horses, their shiny harnesses decorated with silver and brightly colored plumes, lumbered up the drive and stopped beside the front walk. The driver sat quietly, waiting. A black top hat perched jauntily on her head, and her white-gloved hands held the reins gently in her lap.

Howard Butler emerged from one of the bedrooms, his boutonniere in hand. He shook his head and smiled wryly at Tory and Robyn. "If this was a tractor engine, I could manage it," he muttered. "I just can't seem to do this."

Robyn laughed and took the tiny flower arrangement from Tory's dad and deftly pinned it onto the lapel of his suit. She stepped back to admire the effect. "Great," she pronounced. "You're a handsome man, Mr. Butler."

Mr. Butler blushed and smiled, clearly pleased at the compliment.

Tory laughed and slipped her arm through her father's. "OK, Goodlookin', let's go or our carriage might turn into a pumpkin."

"Hi, pretty boys," Tory cooed to the Belgians as they approached the carriage. One of the horses turned his head all the way around as he heard the swish of Tory's full skirt. "It's hard to see with those blinders on, isn't it? Well, it's all right. I'm not going to hurt you."

Mr. Butler helped Tory into the carriage, then climbed in beside her. Robyn slipped into the seat on the other side and straightened Tory's veil. The driver clucked a signal to the team and the carriage lurched forward.

The steep gravel road wound around the hillside and up to an oak grove that shaded the east bank of a small lake. Tory could see Adam standing on a small island in the middle of the lake, the pastor on one side of him and his best man on the other. The flower girl meandered across the wooden bridge that connected the island with the bank, tossing petals onto the bridge and in the water as she walked.

The carriage came to a stop beside a narrow path that led past the rows of seated wedding guests and straight to the wooden bridge. Mr. Butler hopped out of the carriage and helped Tory and Robyn to the ground. Robyn took a deep breath, straightened her shoulders and began to walk slowly toward the bridge. She kept perfect time with the music that wafted over the lake and surrounding hillsides.

"Well, this is it," Mr. Butler whispered. "Are you ready?"

Tory glanced back at the beautiful Belgians standing as if they were posing for a portrait, then at Adam, standing at the end of the bridge with a huge grin on his face.

"Yes," she said, simply. "I am."

The next few hours flew by in a blur of happy moments, one after the other. Tory wished she could keep each one of them in her heart and never forget a single one. She smiled to herself as she pulled them back through her mind one by one: the bullfrog that joined the chorus as Adam's dad sang the Lord's prayer, the look of adoration on Adam's face as they exchanged vows, the delight on the children's faces taking rides in the horsedrawn carriage after the ceremony. . . . She couldn't believe it was all over so soon.

The afternoon sun sank behind the ridge above them as Tory stood with Adam under a flower-entwined bower, sipping punch and munching wedding cake.

Adam leaned over and kissed her, whispering, "Well, Mrs. Hartman, are you ready to head for the north country?"

Tory shivered. "Oooh. In all the excitement I almost forgot about it!" She quickly kissed Adam back. "Yes. I'm ready." She nodded toward the team of Belgians resting in the driveway below them, waiting to be loaded into the long trailer that would take the horses back home. "I just wish we could take those guys with us. Wouldn't they be great for pulling logs out of the woods for firewood for the lodge? We could ride them, too. I wouldn't even be afraid of meeting up with a bear if I was on one of them. They're like Sherman tanks."

Adam slipped his arm around Tory's waist and together they watched as the petite woman who drove the carriage and her strapping young helper loaded one of the Belgians into the trailer. "It *would* be nice to have a team like that," he said, finally. "I wonder if there are any Belgians in northern Idaho for sale."

Just then Tory's parents approached them. Dee Butler kissed her daughter on the cheek and brushed away a tear from her own. "It was beautiful, Tory," she said, dabbing at her nose with a white handkerchief. She waved her arm in a broad semi-circle, taking in the rolling hills and the wild flowers bordering the placid little lake. "You couldn't have picked a more breath-taking spot to have a wedding."

"The valley we're going to in northern Idaho is even more breathtaking than this," Adam spoke up, a tremor of excitement in his voice. "The retreat center's main lodge sits on the edge of a remote valley right on the Canadian border. Julia and Dave—the counselors who direct the center—picked the spot because it is so remote and peaceful. Because it is a place for emotionally hurting people to come to heal and learn how to have healthy relationships, they felt that the setting is most important."

He smiled broadly. "They couldn't have picked a better place. The property is surrounded by Forest Service land and the valley is an animal thoroughfare. The last time I visited up there, I saw several bears searching for grubs out along the creek bank less than a hundred yards from the lodge."

Tory's mom's eyes widened, and she turned to her husband in alarm. "Do you think it's safe for the kids to go up there, Howard?"

Mr. Butler chuckled. "Probably not, Dee," he said, hugging her close. "It's no safer and no more dangerous than anywhere else on this planet. After what they've been through already in Honduras with wild fires and machete-brandishing bandits, I'd say they can handle the presence of a few wild animals."

He held a bulky, clumsily wrapped package out to Adam. "Here, these may make a nice addition to those log walls in your new home. I'll get you some real ones to use later. You have a couple more months until the snow hits."

Tory helped Adam pull the wrapping away and they both gasped in amazement as they saw the gift inside. It was a pair of intricately designed snowshoes. The delicate leather lacing formed a flower pattern near the toe of each snowshoe, and a small tag identified them as the handiwork of the Obidjaun Indian tribe. "These are *perfect,*" Tory sighed. "I can't wait to hang them up in the lodge."

"Wow!" Adam whistled in amazement.

"The women of this tribe do all the handiwork," Mr. Butler explained. It was clear by the twinkle in his clear, gray eyes that he was pleased with his gift. "This flower design is their trademark."

Tory threw her arms around both of her parents. "Thank you," she said. "You couldn't have given us a better gift."

The Belgian waiting in the driveway snorted sharply, and both Tory and Adam turned quickly to see what had startled him. A huge golden dog danced just out of reach of the platter-sized hooves of the massive horse, woofing playfully. A slightly smaller black-and-tan dog joined him.

Adam whistled. "Kodiak! Sardidi! Come here," he called. "Don't tease that horse!"

The dogs stopped in their tracks and perked up their ears. Then, as if in one movement, they bounded toward Adam and Tory, their tongues hanging to one side as they panted up the hill. Adam squatted down and held out his arms. "Come on, guys."

"What a pair!" Mr. Butler grinned and shook his head as the dogs leaped into Adam's arms, knocking him to the ground and licking his face. "Are those yours, Adam?"

Adam laughed and struggled to his feet. He grabbed the dogs by their collars and held them still until they had calmed down. "Yes," he said when he had caught his breath. He gave Tory a long sideways glance. "These are *our* dogs. They're going to Idaho with us."

Tory rearranged the full skirt of her wedding gown so she could squat down and scratch the golden dog behind his ears. "So you're the Kodiak I've been hearing so much about. You're even more beautiful than Adam described you."

She turned to the black and tan female and softly stroked her head. The dog's large dark eyes gazed fondly into hers, and her long, slender tail thumped the ground in excitement. "And you're Sardidi. I know Adam told me your name means 'cool one,' but I don't see anything cool about you. You're a warm-hearted one. I can tell."

"They're hyper right now," Adam said, apologetically. "I had my brother pen them up so they wouldn't disturb the wedding. They feel like they've missed out on all the activity."

Mrs. Butler reached down to pat Sardidi's head and smiled. "No need to apologize for them," she said. "These guys are special." She glanced up at Tory, a look of relief in her eyes. "I'm glad they're going with you to the wilderness. They'll be protection for you when you walk in the woods. I've heard so many stories about mountain lion attacks on people up there in the north country. It feels better to know you'll have such big, strong dogs to go with you."

Tory stood and moved closer to her mother, slipped her arm around her waist, and squeezed her tight. "Don't worry, Mom," she said, laying her head on her mom's shoulder. "Nothing is going to happen to me or to Adam that God can't handle. OK?"

Mrs. Butler sighed. "OK," she whispered. She pushed a stray lock of hair back from Tory's face, tears welling up in her dark eyes. "I guess I'll just have to leave you both in God's hands now, won't I?"

"Yes," Tory said, pecking her mom on the cheek. "I can't think of a safer place to be."

CHAPTER TWO

Tory dozed off and on as the miles disappeared under the tires of Adam's little red Toyota pickup. She stared out the window at the dry landscape of eastern Washington and gulped as she thought of the tears in Robyn's eyes as they hugged after the wedding. The same fear hidden behind her best friend's smile had clouded her mother's face as she waved goodbye.

Adam reached over and took her hand. "What are you thinking about?" he asked quietly. "You seem a million miles away."

"Actually, just a few hundred," Tory said. She squeezed Adam's hand. "I was thinking about how everyone at home has reacted to our going to Idaho. Everyone seems supportive but afraid for us. I'm not sure what to think about it."

Adam laughed. "Aw, they're just jealous because they can't live in the wilderness, too." He glanced over his shoulder through the cab window to check on the dogs and on the trailer that held their belongings. The dogs lay curled up on an old blanket in the back of the pickup. "See, Kodiak and Sardidi know there's nothing to worry about. They're sleeping like babies."

Adam began to hum the tune to one of the praise songs he and Tory had sung together a hundred times in Honduras. Tory smiled and hummed along, then sang out loud as they came to the chorus. She felt the nagging sense of apprehension that gnawed at the corners of her mind melt away as Adam's rich baritone voice filled the cab.

"What a friend we have in Jesus
All our sins and griefs to bear.
What a privilege to carry
Everything to God in prayer. . . ."

Adam stopped singing abruptly and looked over at Tory, his blue eyes sparkling as with an exciting new thought. "Let's pray while we drive. We know we can talk to God about everything that's going on right now. We can tell Him what we're afraid of, what we are dreaming about for this next year in Idaho, what we need, who we have concerns for, *everything.*" He grinned broadly. "Don't you think that would be a great way to start our marriage?"

Tory reached out and touched Adam's face gently. A feeling of deep tenderness and love for him welled up with such overwhelming force that for a moment she couldn't even speak. She thought of the time on the lake in Honduras when Adam had asked her to marry him. She had felt then that she could never love him more than at that moment. But now . . .

"Great idea," she said as she regained her voice. She wanted to try to explain her feelings, but wasn't sure it would even come out right. She just dropped her hand to her lap and smiled at him.

The miles seemed to fly by as Tory took turns praying out loud with Adam. She had heard him pray many times in Honduras, but is seemed different now that they were married. His prayers felt like a warm blanket covering her, holding her up to God in a new way.

It was late afternoon on the second day when they finally pulled into the campground that marked the beginning of the rough road up to the retreat center. A secluded lake surrounded by stately fir and pine trees shimmered in the fading light. Adam lowered the truck's tailgate and let Sardidi and Kodiak out to walk with them around the lake. The dogs shook themselves, then began to sniff the air. Their tails wagged with the pure joy of freedom as they bounded down the path ahead of Tory and Adam.

An osprey screamed from its nest in a tamarack snag at the north end of the lake. It took flight over the lake, then dived down to the surface, its talons outstretched. Snatching a fish from the water, it flew heavily back toward the snag where Tory could see three little heads peeking over the edge of the nest.

"Look!" Tory gasped as a huge eagle, its white tail feathers flashing, plummeted down from the sky toward the osprey. The eagle hit the osprey full force and the fish in the osprey's talons dropped back into the lake with a splash. The eagle swooped to catch the fish and slowly flapped away, the stolen prize firmly grasped in its talons.

Adam stood with his mouth hanging open. "Well, I'll be a monkey's uncle," he said, regaining his composure. "Can you believe what we just saw? Piracy. That's what it was. Pure piracy. And who would have thought that the symbol of our country would do such a thing!"

Tory shook her head in amazement. "And to a mother with hungry children to feed too." She pointed up to the nest where the osprey now roosted.

Just then, Kodiak and Sardidi galloped back up the trail toward them, their thick coats matted with burrs and their paws coated with thick black mud. Sardidi, in her enthusiasm to see Adam, jumped up and planted two muddy forepaws on his chest.

"Sardidi, stop it," Adam scolded. "Ten minutes in the wilderness and you're already acting like a wild animal!"

Tory laughed. "I think we have a couple of very happy kids here." She picked several burrs from behind Kodiak's floppy ears and gazed around at the deep forest surrounding the glassy lake. Massive patches of dainty sky-blue blossoms with bright yellow centers framed the water's edge. A pair of wood ducks paddled placidly across the lake, four half-grown ducklings following them like small, feathered soldiers in formation. She sighed at the utter peacefulness of the scene.

"Well, are you ready to see our new home?" Adam smiled at Tory, a pleased twinkle in his eyes. Tory nodded and walked with Adam back up the trail to the truck.

"I think we'll be spending a lot of time down here at this lake," she murmured happily.

The first half mile of the road to the lodge was straight and fairly smooth. Tory felt her hopes rising that maybe the reports she had heard about the road conditions had been exaggerated. The deeper they traveled into the forest, however, the worse the road got. Deep ruts made progress slow and tedious.

"These ruts are formed during 'breakup,'" Adam explained as he veered back and forth over the road trying to find the smoothest ground. The trailer bounced in and out of the ruts. "The ground freezes in the winter, then thaws in late spring to create a deep layer of soft, wet ground. This road turns into a sea of mud."

Tory stared at Adam. "So how do we get in and out when this happens?"

"With great difficulty." Adam smiled wryly. "Fortunately, breakup only lasts about six weeks in the spring. The worst scenario is when we're in the middle of breakup and we get a late snowstorm. Then we have mud *and* snow." He shuddered at the thought.

The road wound through a stand of aspen, across an old wooden bridge that spanned a rushing creek, then took a sharp left into an open valley. Tall green grass waved in the breeze and bright yellow and white flowers dotted the meadow. A rustic pole barn filled with old machinery nestled in the trees on one side of the entrance. Straight ahead, Tory could see the lodge.

"It's huge!" Tory exclaimed. "And beautiful. Look at those logs. I love all the windows and that deck all the way around the whole building."

As they pulled into the parking area behind the lodge, a tall, dark-haired woman in her early forties wearing a bright-red apron dusted with flour hurried out to meet them. Adam jumped out of the truck and gave the woman a warm hug, then turned to introduce her to Tory.

"This is Julia," he said, as Tory slipped around the truck to stand beside Adam. "Dave, her husband, is in town right now. They are the couple I told you about that are running Border Mountain. We're here to help them."

Tory reached out to shake the woman's hand. "I'm glad to meet you, Julia. This is a beautiful place."

"I'm very glad to meet you, too, Tory," Julia said. She smiled, and Tory noticed that her hazel eyes had flecks of green in them that caught the sunlight. Her long, dark hair pulled into a French braid had streaks of gray in it, but her face lit up with the wonder and excitement of a small child. "Just wait until you see the rest of the place. And the bears. They've been visiting us almost every day. You'll love it here."

Adam caught Tory's eye and winked at her. Tory smiled and winked back. She knew Adam could sense that she liked Julia and it pleased him.

"Come in and see the lodge," Julia said, motioning

toward the door. "We'll help you unload later. Thankfully it gets dark a little later in the summertime so we'll have some light to work by. If this was December we'd be operating by kerosene lamp already."

If the lodge appeared large from the outside, it looked absolutely massive on the inside. The living room faced the meadow with a perfect view of the mountain range beyond through picture windows from the vaulted ceiling to the floor. A tangle of green plants framed the windows and hung from the log rafters, giving the area a homey, inviting feeling.

Tory followed Adam and Julia up a winding log staircase to the upper level of the lodge. Each of the six bedrooms opened out onto a comfortable loft area. Most of them had their own door to the outside with a small deck for privacy. Two bathrooms were located between the bedrooms on opposite sides of the loft.

Julia pushed open one of the bedroom doors. "This will be your room," she said. "It has its own bath and two small decks. It's the largest one in the house besides ours. I thought you'd enjoy the privacy. We have two other clients right now and are expecting a third next week."

Tory caught her breath as she entered the room. A beautiful garden tub with green plants hanging around it occupied an alcove on one side of the room. One deck overlooked the meadow on the west side of the lodge and the other opened out over the woods to the south. She slipped out onto the side deck and took a deep breath of the cool evening air. She could see Kodiak and Sardidi racing through the trees, sniffing at every ground squirrel hole in a frenzy of delight.

Suddenly a sound made her blood seem to freeze in her veins. Almost like the scream of a woman, the cry had a wild and terrifying tone. She turned and ran back into the house, slamming the door behind her, her heart pounding with fear. Instantly, Adam was beside her.

"What was *that?*" Tory wailed, burying her face in Adam's chest. He wrapped his arms around her and held her close until she stopped shaking. Julia reached out and touched Tory's arm.

"It was a mountain lion," she said. "It's OK. They sound a lot worse than they really are."

Tory shuddered, wishing she could shake off her fear like Kodiak and Sardidi shook off water after a swim. "It sounded like it was right beside the house."

Julia nodded. "I know. It very likely was. We have several that live in this area. You probably won't ever see it, though. They're pretty shy."

"Good." Tory took a deep breath and let go of Adam. "OK. I'm ready for the rest of the tour."

They walked through the lodge, then out onto the deck that overlooked the long, narrow valley between the mountains. Two deer grazed at the far end of the valley in the deepening shadows. A flock of Canada geese circled and landed in the beaver pond below the lodge. Just then a large, gangly form appeared at the edge of the woods beyond the pond.

"It's a moose," Adam whispered. "Quiet, everyone. Let's see how long she'll stay there."

They stood stock still as the cow moose edged her way toward the pond, stopping every few feet to sniff the air for any scent of danger. Then she looked back toward the trees and let out a low sound. All at once, two moose calves appeared, their little ears perked forward to catch any signals from their mom. The trio cautiously approached the pond, and the twin calves watched as the cow dropped her head to drink.

Just then, Kodiak and Sardidi bounded around the lodge and caught sight of the moose family. Kodiak let out a howl and bounced stiff-legged down the valley, the ruff on the back of his neck standing straight up at the sight of intruders on his new home turf. Sardidi followed close behind. Her higher pitched bark echoed through the valley, and all the animals immediately scattered.

Julia laughed. "The animals in this valley are in for an adjustment period with these guys around. They'll get used to each other, though. We all coexist pretty well here."

As they turned to go back inside, Tory glanced up at the mountainside where she had heard the mountain lion scream. She thought of her mother's concern for their safety in this wild country.

Father, she prayed silently, *I know You're always with us and will protect us from danger, but thank You for sending Kodiak and Sardidi along.*

CHAPTER THREE

The soft chittering of birds in the trees outside the window awakened Tory from a sound sleep. Never in her life could she remember sleeping so peacefully. Still groggy, she rolled over in bed and reached for Adam. The covers were thrown back, and his side of the bed was empty. She felt a sharp pang in her heart as she realized he had not awakened her when he got up.

Tory sat up straight and grabbed the pair of old jeans she had pulled from her suitcase the night before. "Adam Hartman, you are *not* going exploring without me," she muttered under her breath. She ran a comb through her long, dark hair and pulled it into a ponytail. Pushing her feet into her favorite pair of hiking boots, she laced them tightly.

As she hurried down the log staircase, the sweet smell of pancakes wafted up to meet her. Adam sat at the dining table with a newspaper in his hand. A tall man with a salt-and-pepper beard and a long ponytail sat across from him, pouring syrup on a stack of pancakes. Two other young men hunkered over plates of pancakes, devouring them with gusto.

Adam jumped up as soon as he saw Tory. "Hey, you're awake." He hugged her, then turned to the man at the table. "Dave, this is my wife, Tory."

The man stood up and extended a mammoth hand to

Tory. His handshake was firm, warm, and friendly. The gentle look in his brown eyes reminded Tory of the Belgian horses at the wedding. "Welcome, Tory. We've been looking forward to your arrival," he said, a kind tone in his voice. "It was so late when I got in from town last night I didn't want to wake you two. I figured we'd have plenty of time to get acquainted." He nodded at the two young men. "And this is Kenneth Thomas and his brother, Eric.

Tory nodded to each of the men. "I'm glad to meet you, Dave and Kenneth and Eric."

Just then Julia appeared with a plateful of pancakes, fresh from the griddle. She smiled at Tory. "Feels good to sleep when it's so quiet, doesn't it? Have a seat and dig into a stack of these genuine Idaho flapjacks."

Tory sat down beside Adam, bowed her head for a silent blessing, trying to shove her hurt feelings to the back of her mind, then helped herself to three pancakes, each one of them the size of a plate. She started to pour syrup over her stack when Julia spoke up.

"Wait a minute, Tory," she said, disappearing into the pantry on the far side of the kitchen. "I have a special treat for you to try." She emerged with a jar of dark liquid in her hand and set it on the table in front of Tory and Adam. "It's saskatoon syrup."

Tory reached for the jar and held it up to the light. It was a lovely shade of deep purple. She unscrewed the lid and poured the syrup, thick and rich, over her pancakes. As she lifted the first mouthful of pancake to her mouth, she could smell the syrup. It had a distinct berry scent.

"What's a 'saskatoon'?" she asked after she had finished chewing the first bite of pancake. "The syrup tastes great! Like a cross between blueberries and apples."

Dave laughed. "That's a good description. It's a

berry that grows wild in the North country. In fact, there's a bush of them right out there." He pointed out the window to a tall bush in the meadow by the creek. "You can pick some later and make a pie if you want a real Idaho experience."

"Yeah, right, Mr. Zeilinski," Julia piped up, laughing. "She can make a pie if she *wants* to. I'm sure it wouldn't hurt your feelings a bit if she did."

Dave feigned an innocent look. "No, I don't think it would hurt my feelings."

Then he leaned over to Tory and said, in a staged whisper, "She's right. I *do* love saskatoon pie. And if you made one and happened to offer me a piece, I sure wouldn't turn it down."

By now, Adam, Julia, Kenneth, and Eric were all chuckling heartily. Tory joined in, feeling right at home in the warm, comfortable atmosphere of Julia and Dave's home. She liked both of them and felt sure she would enjoy working with them.

"Hey, listen to this," Adam exclaimed, pointing to an ad in the paper spread before him. "Here's a team of Belgian horses for sale. Seven-year-old geldings that are trained for logging."

Dave leaned over to check out the ad. His eyes lit up with interest as he read. "Golden, British Columbia. Hmm. That's only a couple hours from here." He stood up and walked to the picture window, staring out over the meadow. Then he turned to Julia.

"What do you think, Jules? Wouldn't it be great to have a team of horses here to help with the firewood and work around the place?"

Julia nodded, a thoughtful expression on her face. She tucked a rogue lock of hair behind her ear and flipped two more pancakes onto the platter, tucking a cloth napkin around them before setting the plate on the table. "We could clear the corral and that wooded area just to the north of the lodge," she said. "There's plenty of room in the pole barn to store a winter's supply of hay."

"I'll call the number in the ad right after breakfast," Dave said, a ring of determination in his voice. Tory smiled to herself. She had only known this gentle giant of a man for a few minutes, but she felt sure that once he made up his mind to do something, it would take a pretty powerful force to sway him from it.

As soon as breakfast was over, Kenneth and Eric began to clear the table and stack the dishes in the kitchen sink. Dave ran a basin full of hot soapy water and washed each dish carefully before rinsing it and placing it in the drain tray to air dry. Tory glanced at Julia in surprise, expecting her to protest to Dave that dishes were a woman's job and she'd take care of them while he headed outside to more "manly" tasks. Julia caught Tory's quizzical expression and grinned at her.

"When I cook, he usually washes dishes," she explained. "We all pitch in and do what needs to be done around here. We don't have any set expectations of each other."

Dave nodded in agreement. "We have found that every relationship has an underlying, unspoken theme. Some of the couples that come here to Border Mountain for therapy have adopted a relationship theme of 'abuse.' They don't think about it consciously, but it's what they act out through attempting to control each other. It might be through criticism or some other form of emotional attack. Or it may be through physical violence. Often it happens through one person's withdrawal and cold silence."

"Some take on 'fairness' as their relationship

theme," Julia piped in. "Each one wants to make sure the other is doing their 'fair share.' It sounds OK on the surface, but the problem is that what is fair to one person may seem unfair to the other. Couples who choose this theme do a lot of measuring, trying to make sure the other person is doing their part. Resentment builds up and love is choked out by mental lists and expectations."

Dave moved over close to Julia and put his arm around her shoulder. "The relationship theme *we've* chosen is 'freedom and interdependence.' We each allow the other to be who they are and to do what they need to do to be healthy."

Adam leaned against the kitchen counter, a puzzled expression on his face as he listened. "So, with all this freedom, how do you guys get anything done? How do you know who does what?"

Julia laughed. "Actually, we get *more* done than couples who are trying to control each other, because we don't spend a lot of energy fighting. We allow each other the freedom to take on the daily tasks that best match our personality types and interests and negotiate the ones that neither one of us really wants to do."

"Wow." Tory took a deep breath. She thought of the pain she had felt this morning when Adam got up and started his day without her. Was she trying to control him? "I can see I have a lot to learn from you guys. Is this the kind of stuff you teach in your recovery classes here at Border Mountain?"

Dave looked at Julia and smiled. "Yep. And lots more. It's amazing how quickly people's lives are healed and changed when they understand what's causing their pain and decide to let God do something about it."

Kenneth handed Julia the jar of saskatoon syrup from the table and nodded in agreement. "You don't have to be married to learn about good relationships, either. What I'm learning here about good personal boundaries and being real and honest with myself, and God is already changing the way I relate to my family." He poked Eric in the ribs, grinning mischievously. "Right, bro?"

Eric laughed. "Right."

"Well, that's enough heavy stuff for one breakfast time," Julia pronounced good-naturedly. "Let's make some phone calls. We may be headed for British Columbia this afternoon to expand our family by two new four-footed members."

The afternoon sun beat down on Tory's arm through the open car window as she sat beside Adam in the back seat of Dave and Julia's station wagon headed for Golden, British Columbia. Kenneth and Eric had elected to stay at the lodge to complete some writing assignments before the evening boundaries class. She shook her head with amazement and admiration as she thought of guys so young choosing to learn about forming healthy relationships *before* creating a mess of their lives with poor choices.

Throughout the three-hour car ride to Golden, Tory marveled that the North country could be so hot. Somehow, she had expected cool crisp days of summer giving way to deep snowdrifts in winter. This muggy weather seemed to belong more in Honduras than Canada. She sighed in relief when Dave turned the car into a winding drive up to a rustic cabin in the woods.

"This is it," Dave announced cheerily. "This is where the logger that owns the Belgians lives. I'll go and knock on the door."

The door swung open and a dark-haired young man emerged from the cabin. Dave shook hands with him and talked for a few moments, then motioned to the rest of the group to join them. He pointed to a field across the road from the cabin.

Tory turned to look in the direction Dave pointed and stopped in her tracks. There in the field, standing shoulder to shoulder, were two of the most magnificent Belgian geldings she'd ever seen. The horses' majestically muscled bodies rippled under rich reddish-tan coats and long, flowing white manes.

Tory grabbed Adam's hand and squeezed. "Are these guys incredible, or what?" she whispered. Adam grinned at her, his eyes sparkling with excitement.

The Belgians trotted over to the fence as soon as they saw their master, who introduced himself to the group as Bruce. "No worries, eh mates?" the young man sang out to the horses in his musical Canadian accent. He offered them chunks of apple and carrot from his pockets.

From this close vantage point, Tory could see that one of the horses was bigger and had a thicker chest than the other. He pushed his way ahead of his teammate and claimed the first bites of apple, making it clear that his was the dominant position in this two-horse herd.

"This is Saskatoon," Bruce said proudly, stroking the larger gelding's massive nose. "And this guy is Knick-knick." He pushed Saskatoon aside and offered a carrot piece to the smaller horse. "Knick isn't quite as big as Saskatoon, but his heart makes up for what he lacks in size. You'll see."

Saskatoon, Tory whispered to Julia. "I know what that is, after this morning anyway. This horse is named after a wild berry!"

Julia giggled. "Let's hope he's not as wild as his name," she whispered back. "Actually, Knick-knick is the

Indian name for the bear berries that grow in the meadow, so these guys are *both* named after wild berries."

Adam helped Bruce slip halters over the horses' heads and lead them to the barn where the harnesses hung, freshly oiled, on wooden pegs. Tory watched, fascinated as Bruce lifted the heavy collars onto the horses' necks and slipped the metal hames into place over the collars. He placed the harness over the horses' backs, fastening the long leather shanks he called "traces" to the hames. He attached the whole outfit to a heavy metal bar behind the horses. When the harnessing was completed, he turned to Tory.

"Are you ready to drive them?" he asked. His thick, dark eyebrows raised in amusement as she shrank back.

"Uh, n-no," she stammered. "I've never driven a team before. I don't know how."

Bruce grabbed a crumpled Australian hat from a nail on the barn wall and pulled it down over his head. Then he stepped behind the horses, holding the reins in both hands. "You can do it, miss, no worries. But I'll have a go at a little demonstration. Then whoever would like to try can do so, eh?"

As if by magic, the horses stepped out in perfect unison as soon as Bruce lifted the reins and made a squeaky kissing sound with his mouth. He used voice commands to guide them to a large log in the middle of the field beside the cabin.

"Watch this," he said, proudly, as he chained the log to the iron bar behind the horses. As soon as Saskatoon felt the weight of the log, he arched his neck and lifted his feathered legs high in a prance. Knick-knick craned his neck around first to see what he was pulling, then straightened and leaned into the harness with Saskatoon. Bruce continued to use voice commands to guide them.

"Gee, Sas," he called, signaling the horse on the right to lead out in a right turn. "Haw, Knick," he commanded, and the smaller gelding immediately turned to the left with Saskatoon following his lead. Under Bruce's skilled handling, the horses danced around in tight circles, never tangling in the traces and maneuvering the heavy log behind them as if it were a child's toy.

Dave tried his hand at guiding the horses next, then Adam and Julia followed suit. No matter whose hands held the reins, the huge horses responded with perfect obedience to gentle tugs and crisp voice commands.

"Well, miss. Are you ready for a go?" Bruce pushed his hat back and grinned at Tory. "All the rest survived it. You surely will too, eh?"

Tory stepped forward and took the reins. She made the same kissing sound that she had heard Bruce make. The Belgians moved forward without a second's hesitation, their platter-sized hooves hitting the ground in an almost dance-like rhythm. As long as the reins were, she could feel the tension on the horse's mouth and their responses to the bits. She called out a command and the geldings responded perfectly.

After several rounds of the pasture, Tory brought the horses to a halt in front of the barn. She beamed at Dave and Julia. "Well, I am totally and completely in love," she announced. Then she grinned at Adam. "Not to replace you, of course."

Adam frowned playfully. "Good. I was worried there for a minute that you would forget all about me with these two around." His expression grew serious and Tory wondered as he looked into her eyes if he could read this morning's pain there. He winked at her then, and turned his attention back to the Belgians.

Dave walked around the horses, studying them carefully. Tory knew he was checking them out for any unsoundness. He examined their teeth and ran his hands down their legs, feeling for warmth that might signal inflammation in the joints. He asked Bruce about any bad habits they might have: kicking, cribbing, biting, or barnboundedness. Bruce shook his head "no" to all of Dave's questions.

"Well, I think we're all pretty sold on these guys," Dave said, pulling his checkbook from his pocket. "Let's make it official."

While Dave and Julia negotiated the financial details of the sale with Bruce, Tory and Adam moved in close beside the horses. Tory ran her hand down the crisp white blaze on Saskatoon's face.

"You'll like it at Border Mountain, Sas, I promise," she whispered. "We've got some adventures waiting for us there. Just wait and see."

CHAPTER FOUR

A cool evening breeze blew down the valley, rustling through the tall grass in the meadow and sending the aspens on the mountainside into a shimmering dance. Tory plopped another handful of the rich, deep blue saskatoon berries into the half-filled container tied to her waist.

Two does, each with a half-grown but still-spotted fawn, appeared at the edge of the meadow, moving cautiously upwind, alert for enemies. Tory paused in her picking and watched the deer make their way through the deep grass until they reached the edge of the swamp that marked the Canadian border, just north of the property.

"Hey, Tory."

The sound of Adam's voice from the pole barn pulled her attention from the meadow. She turned to see him walking toward her, leading Saskatoon and Knickknick, Kodiak and Sardidi close at his heels. It had been a week since Bruce had pulled into the driveway towing the long horse trailer that held the Belgians. The horses had seemed relieved to be out of the trailer after their long ride and didn't hesitate to enter the temporary corral Dave had constructed out of a solar electric wire. Just this morning, Tory had helped Adam, Dave, Kenneth, and Eric clear the last section of the permanent corral in the woods beside the lodge, and then watched as the men led the geldings into their new enclosure.

Adam held Saskatoon's reins out to Tory. "Want to take a ride before it gets dark?" he asked. "I found a great new trail this afternoon when Dave and I were out searching for standing dead tamarack to pull in for firewood. I only followed it as far as a berm. I'd like to go on farther. I'm pretty sure it ends up at the lake."

"Sure, I'd like to go." Tory slipped the berry bucket from her waist. "Let me run these berries inside. They're for a pie for Sabbath dinner. Julia told me a new client is coming in tomorrow, and I thought a fresh saskatoon pie would be a great welcome to Border Mountain."

Adam grinned. "Good idea. The rest of us won't mind sharing it, either."

"By the way," said Tory, with a quizzical look, "what's a berm?"

"It's the dirt that's piled up when Forest Service workers dig a deep hole in a road or a trail to keep people from driving vehicles on it. The one we saw was about six feet deep and covered the whole width of the road. You'll see it when we ride."

The shrill ringing of the phone brought Tory to quick attention. "I have to run and answer that," she said. "Kenneth and Eric went to town with Julia and Dave to pick up some diesel for the generator and other supplies. That could be the new client calling."

Tory clasped the berry bucket to her chest to keep the fruit from spilling and ran toward the lodge. Kodiak sat down beside Adam and watched her, but Sardidi ran along beside her, not wanting to be left out of anything. She heard several more rings as she and Sardidi reached the porch, but when she burst into the kitchen where the radio phone hung in a leather sling on a log pillar, there was only silence. She picked up the phone.

"Hello, Border Mountain," she said, in her most

professional voice. The only sound she heard was the deep buzz of the dial tone.

"I missed it," she lamented to Adam as she stepped out onto the porch. "I hope it wasn't too important."

The phone rang again and Tory wheeled around, racing for the door. "I'll get it this time!"

Again the kitchen was silent, and all she heard as she picked up the phone was the dial tone. Puzzled, she walked slowly back outside to the place where Adam and Kodiak waited with the horses.

Suddenly the loud ring sounded again, but this time from right behind them. Tory peered up into one of the aspen trees that stood in the yard beside the lodge. There, perched on the top branch, sat a mockingbird.

"You! It was you all along!"

The bird let out another shrill call that sounded exactly like the ring of the phone, then flew away. Tory stared after it, her mouth hanging open in disbelief. "I've been had," she said, shaking her head. "Had by the phone bird."

Adam's sides shook with laughter. "You should have seen your face," he chortled. "That was priceless."

Adam led Saskatoon over to a tall flat-topped stump so that Tory could climb up on the horse's bare back. Then he led Knick-knick to the same stump and used it to vault himself up.

"Wow. These guys are *tall.*" Tory leaned over and looked down at the ground far below. "I don't think I've ever been on a horse this big. I hope he isn't into bucking. It's a long way to the ground."

Adam nodded. "It is, isn't it?" He clucked to Knick-knick and plow-reined him around in a circle. "It's hard to get used to pulling on the rein in the direction I want him to go instead of neck-reining," he said. He urged the mammoth horse into a trot and headed for the meadow with both dogs close at Knick-knick's heels, their tails wagging with delight at the prospects of a walk.

Tory leaned forward and gripped a handful of Saskatoon's thick mane before loosening up on the reins. Saskatoon needed no encouragement. He lunged forward, moving immediately into a long, smooth trot to catch up with his teammate.

Squeezing the horse's sides tightly with her legs to keep her balance at first, Tory soon found that she could relax and enjoy the ride. Saskatoon's smooth gait and wide, comfortable back felt more like sitting in a rocking chair than riding a horse. She patted the gelding's muscular neck.

"You are some horse," she murmured. "I think I'm going to really like riding you."

The trail through the forest began wide, then narrowed until the horses were forced to push through heavy foliage to stay on the path. Tory ducked low on Saskatoon's back, burying her face in his mane to keep from being scrubbed off by the rough branches. She could hear a rushing creek somewhere to their right, so she knew they were still headed in the right direction. The lake lay in a small valley about a mile and a half ahead. The dogs made a wide circle through the woods ahead of them, checking occasionally to be sure they hadn't turned back.

As they broke into a clearing, Adam reined Knick-knick to a stop. He pulled the horse up close beside Saskatoon and leaned over to give Tory a kiss. "Doing OK?"

Tory hesitated. She wanted to talk to Adam about that first morning here at Borden Mountain when he got up and left her and about the insecurity that she felt at other times when he stayed out so long with Dave and left her by herself. She felt silly and petty to be worried about such a thing when the work he was doing with Dave was so important. A ray from the setting sun filtered through the branches of the trees above and enveloped Adam like a rosy halo. She thought of all the adventures she'd shared with him in Honduras. How he'd been there for her, supporting and encouraging her no matter what the circumstances. She couldn't imagine life without him.

"Yep," she said, wishing she could tell him how she felt, but not quite sure how to put it into words. "Just fine and dandy."

The trail widened and began to look like it had once been a road. The horses picked up their pace. They seemed happy to be on an easier trail where they didn't have to fight the underbrush with every step.

"It's not much farther to the lake," Adam called back to Tory, glancing at the red glow spreading across the western sky. "We're going to have to hurry or we'll get caught in the dark. Let's canter a little."

Tory giggled as Saskatoon broke into a rolling gallop. She gripped tight with her knees and twisted the horse's thick mane around both of her hands to hold on. Just ahead the trail curved sharply to the left. She held her breath and leaned into the turn, balancing her body to move with the horse beneath her.

"Look out!" she heard Adam shout as she rounded the curve. There just ahead on the path was a deep hole cut across the width of the trail. She watched in horror as Knick-knick reached the edge of the hole, stumbled and toppled in, his legs flying in the air as he somersaulted. Tory caught a glimpse of Adam's face as he disappeared into the hole under the massive horse.

The berm. Oh, God, no!

Tory heard someone screaming as she pulled Saskatoon to a stop just before the hole. It took her a moment to realize that the voice she heard was her own. An image of Adam's body, mangled and broken, crushed under the weight of the huge horse, flashed into her mind. She was certain that neither Saskatoon nor Adam could have lived through that horrible fall.

Tory slipped from Saskatoon's back and climbed the dirt bank to the edge of the hole just as Knick-knick's head appeared over the bank. With a mighty lunge, he scrambled out of the hole and stood shaking on the path beside Saskatoon.

Just then Adam's face appeared at the edge of the berm. "I'm OK," he said, his voice trembling. He clawed his way out of the hole and sat down on the dirt pile with his head in his hands. Tory moved quickly to his side, slipping her arms around his shoulders, silent tears streaming down her cheeks.

"I thought you were dead," she whispered.

Adam shook his head slowly from side to side. "So did I." He hugged her close. "I'm all right, though. I don't know how, but I am. I felt Knick-knick roll over me while I was still on his back. I should have been squashed under him. But I didn't feel anything. All I can figure out is that my angel must have been working overtime again."

He stood up and walked over to Knick-knick, who had moved to the side of the trail and begun munching on a clump of clover. Tory followed close behind him and held the horse's reins while Adam ran his hands down each of his legs, checking for injuries. The only thing he could find was a small scratch on the end of the horse's nose.

A cool wind rose, puffing its chilly breath across Tory's neck. She shivered and looked around for the first time since the accident. Long shadows crept from the deep forest, snuffing the last thin rays of waning light from the trail. An owl hooted from somewhere on the hillside.

"I think it's time to go home," she said, handing Knick-knick's reins to Adam and pulling the reluctant Saskatoon from the clover patch.

Sensing the apprehension in Tory's voice, Adam moved to her side and took her hand. "Let's lead the horses home," he said quietly. "It will give us a chance to have some prayer time."

Tory nodded and squeezed his hand. "OK," she replied, with more enthusiasm than she felt. She pressed close to Adam as they walked. The rise and fall of Adam's voice as he prayed out loud felt comforting, like the sound of ocean waves lapping against a familiar shore. Yet she didn't really hear any of the words.

Father, she prayed silently, *I can't talk out loud to you about how I'm feeling about this strange and frightening place, about my feelings, about Adam . . . I don't even understand it myself.*

CHAPTER FIVE

A sleek white van inched its way up the rutted drive just as Tory hung the last pair of jeans on the makeshift clothesline Dave had strung between two pines to the north of the lodge. Although it was still early in the day, the sun shone brightly over the eastern mountains. Tory inspected her work with a satisfied smile. Even the heaviest jeans would be dry by mid-afternoon in the crisp, dry air.

Saskatoon nickered to her from the corral. "Not now, boy," Tory called. "We have company and I need to greet them. I'll have a treat for you later."

The van pulled into the parking area in front of the lodge and a lovely slender young woman with short dark hair stepped out from the driver's side. Tory hurried to meet her. Just as she rounded the front of the van and came face to face with the woman, she let out a shriek.

"Breeze!"

"Tory! I didn't know you were here," the young woman gasped. She threw her arms around Tory and gave her a bear hug.

Tory returned the hug, then stepped back, holding her old friend at arm's length. "You look wonderful. Just the same—you haven't changed a bit."

Pain flashed into Breeze's eyes and she looked down quickly, biting her lip. "I feel as if I've changed," she said quietly. She turned to open the sliding door of the van, pulling a large duffel bag and a backpack from the seat. "But there will be plenty of time for talk later. Do you know where I'll be staying? Where's everyone else? Is your new hubby here too? When will I get to meet him?"

"Dave and Julia took Adam with them into town this morning." Tory reached for the duffel bag. "They'll be back sometime this afternoon. I'll show you your room. I have it all ready for you. I just had no idea when I prepared it that it was for *you.*"

Breeze's face lit up as Tory led her through the lodge and up the log staircase to her room. "This is more beautiful than I imagined." She sighed. "And it's so *quiet* here. I love it."

Tory set the duffel bag on the floor at the end of the rustic log bed. She watched as Breeze examined every corner of the cozy room, running her fingers along the gnarled wood of the headboard and across the soft, Pendleton wool blanket on the bed, picking up the kerosene lamp and sniffing its chimney, and gazing in wonder at the Native American paintings on the walls. Finally she sat down on the bed and looked up at Tory.

"It feels safe here," she said, tears filling her eyes.

Tory sat down on the bed beside her friend. "What happened, Breeze? Where's Brian?" She thought of the pain she had felt so long ago when she had learned of Breeze and Brian's relationship. The memories seemed like something she'd read in a book now, she felt so far removed from those days. Her life with Adam filled her thoughts so completely that she had almost forgotten her pain at losing Brian.

Breeze held up her left hand. A dazzling wedding ring sparkled in a shaft of sunlight that streamed through the bedroom window. Tory caught her breath.

"Oh, my. That's a gorgeous ring."

Breeze nodded. "It is, isn't it?" She pulled it from her finger and set it gently on the bedside stand. "I think I'll leave it there for a couple weeks, though. I have a lot of sorting out to do and it will just distract me. I want to talk about all of it. Just not right now." She stood up quickly. "What I'd really like is a tour of Border Mountain. Will you take me on one?"

"Sure," Tory said. "Follow me."

After showing Breeze around the lodge, Tory took her outside to meet Saskatoon and Knick-knick. "We have two big dogs, Kodiak and Sardidi, too," she said, looking around the yard. "They must be out exploring right now. You can meet them later. The horses won't mind having the attention all to themselves for awhile anyway."

She pulled some apple chunks from her pocket and handed them to Breeze. Saskatoon leaned as far as he could reach over the gate at the entrance to the corral, trying to get to the apple pieces before Knick-knick could. Breeze laughed and let Saskatoon have the first few pieces.

"Now it's Knick's turn," she said firmly when he had finished nuzzling the apple slices out of her hand. "Move aside, big boy, and give your buddy a chance for some goodies."

Tory watched Breeze as she interacted with the horses, marveling at her ease and sensitivity around them.

"They're amazing. I love just being close to them," Breeze said as she ran her hand along the arch of Knick-knick's neck. She leaned close to the horse and took a deep breath. "He smells *so* good. I'll never forget that smell."

Tory stood quietly, not wanting to interrupt Breeze's time of bonding with the Belgians. A thousand questions churned in her mind that she longed to ask Breeze, but she kept silent.

"Could we take a ride?" Breeze asked.

"I don't see why not. It would be a great way to show you the rest of the property." Tory leaned over to pull a burr from Saskatoon's forelock, then fed half of the apple slices still left in her pocket to Knick-knick and half to Saskatoon. "How about it guys? Are you up for a jaunt?"

Tory ran back to the garage and took two colorful lead ropes from a peg on the wall. She grabbed the horse's bridles and a couple of hoof picks and brushes. Once back at the corral, she tossed a lead rope, one of the brushes, and a hoof pick to Breeze. She clipped her lead rope to Saskatoon's halter and waited while Breeze fastened the other one to Knick-knick's. Then she opened the corral gate and led Saskatoon out into the yard.

Saskatoon stood quietly while Tory brushed him down, then lifted each foot obediently on command for her to clean out the debris that had collected in them since Adam last cleaned them out. Breeze watched Tory's every move and repeated each one on Knick-knick.

"These guys' hooves are getting long," Tory said. She dropped the last hoof to the ground. She lifted the feathery hairs that grew over the top of Saskatoon's hoof. "And look here, Breeze. This coronet band is looking dry and could start cracking. We need to put some hoof salve on it. This is where the hoof growth starts—any problems here could cause cracks later."

Breeze nodded, listening carefully. She flashed Tory a look of admiration. "I wish I knew as much as you do about horses," she said, a wistful tone in her voice.

"You're good with them, Breeze."

Tory looked at Breeze closely. Something seemed

different about her than she remembered from their days at Cool Springs Camp. She had always admired Breeze's confident attitude. Now she seemed deflated and unsure.

The grooming completed, the girls bridled the horses and led them over to the big stump on the other side of the lodge to mount up. Saskatoon shied to the side as Tory swung her leg up and over, almost spilling her. She grabbed the gelding's mane and steadied herself.

Breeze laughed. "There's a lot more at stake if you fall off these guys," she said. She shifted into a comfortable position on Knick-knick's broad back. "My, but it's a long way to the ground."

Tory took the lead on Saskatoon and reined him through the aspen grove to the north of the lodge and down a hidden trail to the Canadian border. Saskatoon kept one ear pointed forward down the trail and the other cocked back in her direction. He arched his neck and pranced through the undergrowth, clearly pleased to be free of the confinement of the corral. Breeze followed closely on Knick-knick.

A sudden whirring in the undergrowth next to the trail set Saskatoon back almost on his haunches, with Knick-knick piling up behind him.

"Wh-what was that?" Tory gasped. Then she saw a male ruffed grouse where he had flown from his hiding place beside the trail. His neck was puffed up and his tail feathers spread out into a beautiful fan. He strutted through a small clearing beside the path, making deep chuckling noises in his throat.

Breeze leaned forward on Knick-knick's neck, clearly enthralled with the show the little grouse was putting on. "There's got to be a girl grouse around here somewhere," she whispered. "He's not doing this just for us."

"I'm sure there is," Tory whispered back, "but we'll never see her. She blends in with the undergrowth so perfectly, she's virtually invisible."

Within minutes, the grouse completed his dance and disappeared into the brush. The tiny clearing stood empty with no sign that anything had ever happened there.

"Well! That was amazing." Breeze let out a deep breath. "Is this how life in the wilderness is—an incredible surprise around every turn in the path?"

Tory grinned at her friend. "So far it seems to be that way," she said. Her smile faded as she thought of Adam's brush with death the day before. "Some of the surprises aren't fun, though."

Breeze glanced away quickly, tears glistening in her eyes. "I know about that kind of surprise," she said softly.

Tory opened her mouth to ask a question, then closed it again. *Father, I don't know what is bothering Breeze so much,* she prayed silently, *but I know You do. Give her the courage to speak of it when the time is right, and give me the wisdom to support her without pushing her until she's ready to talk.*

Breeze clucked to Knick-knick and reined him back into the trail. Saskatoon fell in right behind him, then pushed his way around him, unwilling to let Knick-knick get ahead of him.

"Sorry," Tory said, flashing Breeze a look of mock helplessness. "Saskatoon just made an administrative decision without consulting me first. He thinks he's the boss around here."

Before Breeze could answer, Saskatoon suddenly shied sideways in the trail, snorting with alarm. Knick-knick squealed and crow-hopped. Tory caught a glimpse of the panic on Breeze's face as Knick-knick ploughed into the black muck of a swampy area on the other side of the trail.

"Hang on to his mane!" Tory shouted. "Try to rein him in!"

Knick-knick plunged on, lunging wildly to free himself from the sucking black mud. Breeze clung to his back with her hands wrapped in his thick mane. Her eyes were wide with fear and all the color had drained from her face.

Just then a sound like a woman screaming rent the air. Saskatoon reared up and pawed the air, then stood trembling with every muscle tensed to bolt. Tory leaned in close to his left ear and talked to him soothingly. She took several deep breaths, trying to calm the pounding in her own heart.

Knick-knick, with one final desperate lunge, pulled himself from the quagmire and back onto the trail. He hung his head low, his sides heaving and foamy sweat covering his quivering chest. Breeze slipped from his back and led him over to the spot where Saskatoon stood with Tory still perched on his back.

"I give," Breeze said, her voice quavering with emotion. "What is out in those woods that makes a noise like that?"

CHAPTER SIX

Tory eased to the ground, careful not to spook Saskatoon anymore. She stood next to Breeze and peered up the mountainside into the thick, dark woods from which the chilling scream had come. With all her heart she wished that Kodiak and Sardidi had accompanied them on this ride.

"Julia told me it's a mountain lion," she said, trying to keep her voice calm and even. She could tell by Breeze's pinched expression and wide eyes that she was on the verge of bolting.

Breeze gulped. "H-how far away do you think this mountain lion is? That scream sounded like it was right beside us. Do you think it will attack?"

Tory shook her head. "No, I don't think so. The horses are too big. From what I've read about them, they like smaller prey unless they're really, really hungry. I heard that if you *are* attacked by a mountain lion that you should stand on your tiptoes and wave your arms in the air, making yourself look as big as possible to intimidate them."

"Oh," Breeze said, wincing. "I hope I don't ever have to test the theory."

"Let's just lead these guys back to the lodge and take a tour of the property another time when the dogs can go with us," Tory suggested. She reached up and smoothed her hand down Saskatoon's sweaty neck. "Is that all right with you, big guy?"

As they walked slowly and silently back down the path to the lodge, the Belgians followed, as calm now as if nothing had ever happened. Tory tried to put the sound of the mountain lion's cry out of her mind. They had almost reached the aspen grove when Breeze broke the silence.

"I don't know what to do with all the fear I have, Tory," she blurted out. "Hearing that mountain lion scared me, but as I felt the fear back there, I realized that it's nothing new for me. I live that way all the time."

Tory listened without responding, waiting for Breeze to go on. Knick-knick nudged Breeze in the back with his nose as he plodded along behind her. She looked startled, chuckled, then became sober again as she continued speaking.

"Life with Brian has been a nightmare for me. Everything seemed so wonderful at first. He seemed so devoted to me and wanted to get married right away. My parents begged me to give it more time, but I was determined to go ahead with the wedding. I guess they saw the warning signs I didn't see. His possessiveness. His temper. The way he blamed other people for his problems instead of owning up to them himself. The way he always needed to be in control." She stared at the ground as she talked, her voice heavy with pain. "It didn't take long for me to realize that I'd made a big mistake."

A raven flapped his way to a treetop beside the path just ahead, tormented by a flock of impertinent jays. A tiny black squirrel chattered insults from a rotten tree stump. Tory led Saskatoon over to a fallen log beside the trail and looped his reins over a gnarled branch stub. She motioned for Breeze to join her.

"We can sit here and talk instead of going back to the lodge right now," she suggested. Breeze nodded and tied Knick-knick to a nearby sapling. She climbed up on the log, sitting cross-legged beside Tory.

"Brian didn't start hitting me right away," she said, her voice strangely distant, as if she were talking about someone else. "He just seemed disgruntled with me all the time. I couldn't do anything right. The house was never clean enough, and he hated the way I managed money. I'd get a job and he'd tell me I wasn't doing enough at home and badger me until I quit. Then he'd accuse me of not doing my share in earning income and blame me for our financial problems."

She sighed heavily. "Before he started hitting me, I kept telling myself it was the stress he was under and things would get better. But they just kept getting worse. No matter what I did, he got angry. He'd wake me up in the middle of the night to yell at me. Sometimes he'd pull the covers off and start hitting me on my legs and back in places where the bruises wouldn't show."

Tory drew in a sharp breath. "Breeze, I had no idea," she said. Her voice felt tight and dry as she spoke. She tried to comprehend gentle, funny Brian treating anyone in such a manner, but she couldn't imagine it. "It all sounds so horrible. Did you talk to anyone about it?"

Breeze shifted her position on the log, drawing her knees up under her chin and wrapping her arms around her legs. She began to shake uncontrollably as tears rolled down her cheeks. "I tried, Tory," she whispered. "No one believed me. I went to our pastor, and he told me I must be doing something to set him off and that I needed to pray more and trust God. He said it was my duty to stand by him no matter how he acted. I felt so trapped and hopeless. Then someone in our church told me about this place. She must have noticed something strange about the way Brian treated me, even though I tried to hide it. She just slipped me a Border Mountain brochure and whispered that she thought maybe I needed some time away to think and pray in a safe place."

Tory reached over and put her arms around her friend's shoulders. "It took a lot of courage for you to come here and get some help," she said, softly. "I'm proud of you."

Breeze smiled through her tears. "I have my work cut out for me, I know. But I want to get better. I want to learn how to set healthy boundaries for myself and to figure out what to do with my marriage. I know God led me here. He'll help me untangle this mass of knots that my life has become."

Just then Kodiak and Sardidi snuffed their way up the trail, their noses fixed on the ground, following the scent of the horses. They soon spotted the girls sitting on the log, and bounded over to them, their tails wagging wildly. Breeze's face lit up and she jumped off the log to greet the dogs.

"Oh, I *love* them," she cried, wrapping her arms around each of their necks and burying her face in Kodiak's thick coat. "They're so *big.*"

Tory squatted down beside Breeze and patted the two truants. "Where were you guys when we *needed* you?" she scolded, playfully. Sardidi reached over and licked Tory's face as if to apologize. "OK. You're forgiven," she said, scratching the dog behind her floppy ears.

Just then Adam appeared on the trail, still dressed in his khakis and dress shirt from the town trip. "Did you need me too?" he asked, his eyes dancing mischievously. Tory had been holding the emotion of the past half-hour inside trying to be strong for Breeze, but as soon as she saw Adam, she felt as if something inside her was crumpling up like an old paper bag. Hot tears filled her eyes and she ran to him.

"Hey, I'm glad to see you too," he said as he hugged her close. "I didn't think I was gone that long." He held her out at arm's length and studied her face. "What happened?"

Breeze stood up. "It was a mountain lion. It screamed from close by up in the woods and spooked the horses. Spooked us too." She held out her hand to shake with Adam. "I'm Breeze," she said with a tired smile.

Adam's face lit up as he took Breeze's hand. Tory could tell that he was surprised at Breeze's stunning good looks. She felt her stomach twist into a knot and suddenly she felt nauseated. Adam didn't seem to notice.

"I'm so glad to meet you," he said, still holding Breeze's hand. "You must be the new client we were expecting today."

Tory, trying to regain her composure, grabbed Adam's arm. She felt as small and insignificant as she had that first summer at Cool Spring camp when beautiful Jan Cole had stolen all the boys' hearts right under her nose. Only this wasn't just any boy. This was *Adam*. She gulped. "Adam. Breeze is my friend. We worked together at Cool Springs camp in Florida four years ago. Isn't that awesome? I never dreamed *she* was the new client!"

"Amazing," Adam said. "How did you find Border Mountain all the way from Florida?"

Breeze slipped her arm around Tory's waist. "God led me here," she said, a new strength in her voice. Tory squeezed her friend close, trying to ignore the ache in her heart.

Back at the lodge, Tory and Breeze brushed the Belgians down, cleaned out their hooves, then ran a tank of fresh water and tossed them a bale of hay. Julia and Dave came out to introduce themselves and hear the story of the mountain lion scare.

Dave rubbed his bearded chin, his face sober as he listened to Tory's account of the morning's happenings.

"I think it's important that we always take the dogs along on walks," he said. "I don't think we're in any real danger, but last winter was the harshest one we've had in more than 30 years. Many of the deer in this area got caught in the deep snow and starved, so the deer population is down dramatically. That means it's slim pickings for the mountain lions. They may act in uncharacteristic ways if they get hungry enough."

Julia slipped one arm around Breeze and one around Tory. "I'm glad you're safe." She gave them both a squeeze. "This is wild country in a lot of ways, but God is faithful. He is bigger than a mountain lion or any other problem we may face here."

Adam nodded thoughtfully as he listened. "It's true," he said quietly. "He's already spared my life once since we've been here. I guess we can trust Him with everything else too."

Dave walked over to the horse's water tank and pulled the black plastic pipe up out of the water to check the flow. Barely a trickle dripped out the end.

"Uh-oh," he groaned. "Speaking of problems, I think we've got one." He traced the black pipe back to the spigot next to the lodge, checking for leaks and cracks. Then he gazed up the mountainside, a look of consternation on his face.

"Adam, if you can change into some grubbies, I need you to go with me up the mountain. Something has cut off the water flow from the spring and we'll have to trace the pipe up to the top to find out what it is."

Breeze's eyes widened in surprise. "Do you mean that all your water here comes from a spring up on the mountain?"

Dave nodded. "Yep. And all the animals in the area know where the pipe is. They hear the water flowing through it even though we've buried it under the ground. They just dig down and chew through it to get a drink."

"Sometimes trees fall near the line and when their roots pull out of the ground, they uproot the line with them," Julia added. She laughed. "With no electricity, wood heat, and this high maintenance water line, I think we spend more time just trying to survive here than doing anything else."

Adam grinned like a little boy. "I love it! Real pioneers."

Dave chuckled. "That's about the size of it. And if we don't get up that mountain and find the leak in our water line, these pioneers are going to get pretty thirsty."

As the guys disappeared into the lodge to change, Julia picked up a stack of berry buckets propped next to the woodshed. "Are you girls up for a berry picking expedition?" she asked, her eyes twinkling. "I know where we can find a clearing loaded with elderberries just waiting to be harvested."

Tory and Breeze both nodded eagerly and took the buckets Julia held out to them. They followed her across the meadow, along the edge of the rushing creek at the edge of the forest, and into the woods at the north end of the valley. Kodiak and Sardidi trailed along, making a wide circle of their own, exploring every ground squirrel den along the way.

The woods, even now with the sun at its peak, seemed dark and ominous to Tory. Downed trees lay haphazardly over the forest floor, like fallen soldiers in some strange wilderness war with the elements. The mountainside jutted almost straight up to the west of the winding animal trail they followed. She stared at the misshapen trunks of the young aspens that managed to survive in the midst of towering tamaracks.

"What bends those trees like that?" she asked Julia as she hurried to catch up with her on the trail.

"Snow," Julia replied. "Lots of snow." She pointed up the mountainside. "The drifts push down on the young trees winter after winter, bending their trunks down. They're determined to reach the sunlight though. They keep reaching for the sky and grow straight up anyway. After a few years their trunks are strong enough to withstand the weight of the snowdrifts, but the early damage remains. They will bear the marks of their struggle for the rest of their lives."

"Kind of like us," Tory heard Breeze whisper behind her.

Yes, kind of like us, Father, Tory thought. *Please help Breeze to keep reaching for You in spite of the pain she's going through. Help her to find healing in the sunlight of Your presence.* She shuddered as she thought of the struggle she'd had on the trail this morning with her feelings about Breeze. *And help me to find that healing too.*

CHAPTER SEVEN

The narrow path through the forest suddenly widened into a clearing dotted with craggy stumps from an old logging foray. Bright blue lupine and blood-red paintbrush splashed their vibrant color across the open meadow, bringing new life to the scene of destruction. Bear berries, late summer strawberries, and huckleberries grew in profusion in the bright late-summer sunshine. Tory took a deep breath as she stood with Breeze and Julia at the edge of the clearing.

"It's beautiful." She gave Julia a quizzical look. "Would any of these berries be growing here if they hadn't logged this?"

Julia shook her head. "No," she said. "These berries require more sunlight than they could get in the forest. As sad as it is that the trees were cut down, the logging operation here created a meadow that provides food for hundreds of creatures." She glanced at Breeze. "Kind of a life lesson, isn't it? Sometimes the things that make us feel the most destroyed contain the seeds for the greatest growth and good."

Breeze nodded. She bent down and picked a stalk of lupine that bloomed at the base of an old stump. "I'm going to dry this and keep it in my journal," she said. "I have a feeling I'll need it as a reminder in the months to come."

Julia led the way to a stand of elderberry bushes,

loaded with clusters of tiny, silver-coated purple berries. She showed Tory and Breeze how to pick the ripest, most juicy berries without bruising or crushing them. Soon all their buckets were full.

"I guess we needed more buckets," Julia said, laughing. "I knew the berries were good this year, but I had no idea we'd find such a bumper crop. Next time we can wear backpacks lined with garbage bags. We'll have no trouble filling them up."

Breeze peered into her bucket at the clumps of miniature berries. "What do you do with elderberries after you get them home?"

"Jam, syrup, pies, juice—you name it," Julia replied. "I combine them with crabapples because elderberries by themselves don't have enough acid to keep them from spoiling once they're canned. It's a dynamite combination. Just wait 'til you taste it."

Tory felt her stomach rumbling as she listened. She realized suddenly that neither she nor Breeze had remembered to eat lunch in all the excitement over the mountain lion and the broken water line. She picked a handful of elderberries from their stem and popped them into her mouth. The berries had a tangy, tart flavor that reminded her of rhubarb crossed with grapes.

"Ready to head back?" Julia hoisted her bucket and turned toward the place where the path entered the edge of the woods. "Where are the dogs? I thought they were with us, but I haven't seen them since we entered the woods. Off on a hunting expedition of their own, I guess."

Breeze giggled. "I'll bet *they* aren't looking for berries."

She followed Julia through the meadow with Tory bringing up the rear. A red-tailed hawk circled the field overhead, hunting for small rodents. As she walked

Tory watched the graceful bird until the trees blocked her view.

Suddenly the air was filled with frantic barking. Tory recognized Kodiak's deep, woofing bark and Sardidi's shrill, high-pitched tones. The barking seemed to come from somewhere in the forest and grew steadily closer. The women stood as if rooted to the ground.

Just then the dogs appeared in the path ahead, racing through the forest with their tails tucked tightly between their legs. A hundred yards or so behind them, in hot pursuit, was a grizzly sow. Tory gasped and dropped to the ground. She knew that she was no match for a full-grown grizzly who could run up to 35 miles an hour and climb any tree she could.

"God help us," she heard Julia whisper as the dogs raced around behind her and sat down whimpering, as if waiting for her to protect them from the monster chasing them.

As soon as the grizzly spotted the three humans, she stopped abruptly and stood up on her hind legs, sniffing the air and weaving her head back and forth.

Julia crouched low and motioned to Tory and Breeze to do the same. "Don't move," she whispered. "Bears are just the opposite of mountain lions. If she attacks, lay totally still face-down on the ground and cover the back of your neck with your hands."

Tory nodded and noticed that, although Breeze's hands were trembling, a look of quiet trust filled her eyes.

As the bear hesitated, apparently confused at this unexpected turn of events, something rustled in the undergrowth behind her. A lanky cub appeared, mewling his displeasure to his mother for running off and leaving him. He soon spotted the women and stood on his hind legs in perfect mimic of his mother, staring at them curiously.

"So you're a mom," Tory whispered. "No wonder you were chasing the dogs with such a vengeance. You were protecting your baby."

The mother bear dropped to all fours and grunted a warning to her cub. Then, as suddenly as she had appeared, she disappeared into the forest, the youngster tumbling at her heels. As soon as they were gone, Kodiak and Sardidi jumped up from their hiding place behind Julia.

"You . . . you *scoundrels!*" Julia scolded them, sinking to the ground in sheer relief and letting the dogs lick her face and neck. "Are you trying to get us all killed? Huh?"

Kodiak sat down and extended a paw to Julia to shake. She hugged him and laughed. "All right. I'm sure you didn't mean to aggravate that old mamma bear."

She turned to Tory and Breeze. "Are you guys OK?"

"Yes, I think I am," Breeze said as she collapsed onto a patch of soft, green moss. "I've only been here one day and I've already been threatened by a mountain lion and accosted by a grizzly bear. What kind of place is this?"

Julia sat silently for a long time before answering. When she spoke, there was a note of deep conviction in her voice. "It's a sink-or-swim kind of place, I think. We either trust God to take care of us day to day, or we drown in fear. It's as simple as that. We survive every day on trust." She smiled at Breeze. "You did well. I could see on your face that you weren't panicking."

"I don't know why I didn't," Breeze said, dropping her eyes shyly. "It just seemed as if God was right here beside me, telling me everything was going to be all right. It was like I could hear the words, 'I will keep him in perfect peace whose mind is stayed on Me' echoing through my mind." She looked up at Tory and grinned. "I think I'm really beginning to learn to believe Him."

All the way back to the lodge, Kodiak and Sardidi stayed close at Tory's heels. They refused to be lured away even by the shrill, teasing whistle of a black squirrel in a nearby snag. Julia walked quickly, singing hymns as she strode through the dark woods. Breeze joined her, harmonizing the lower alto part with Julia's high soprano. Tory knew that the chances of encountering another bear on their way home were slim, but it felt somehow comforting to hear the lilting music and know that it served to warn away any animals in the area.

Saskatoon and Knick-knick whinnied a greeting to the three hikers as they broke out of the woods and into the Border Mountain valley. Tory could see all four men in the wood lot hunkered over a chainsaw. They looked up and waved as they saw the women approaching. Julia held up her bucket of berries and let out a whoop of victory.

"We found *tons* of berries," she shouted. "We *scored.*"

Dave nodded and waved again, flashing Julia a grin. He set his tools down and walked out into the meadow to meet them, Adam close at his heels.

"Wow," he said as he looked into their buckets. "You *did* score, didn't you?" He noticed the dogs trailing behind Tory. "Good, I'm glad you had the dogs with you. I was worried."

Julia laughed. "A lot of good they did us. They almost got us eaten by a grizzly." She blurted out the whole story of the mother bear and Kodiak and Sardidi's antics.

Adam moved quickly to Tory's side and held her close as Julia talked. He looked especially alarmed when Julia got to the part about the cub. "God was surely with you," he said, his voice choking with emotion. "Mother bears are known for their horrible tempers when they feel that their cubs are threatened."

"I know," Julia said quietly, glancing at Breeze and Tory. "We were protected."

That night, after a supper of lentil soup and cornbread with thick slices of saskatoon pie for dessert, Tory snuggled down on the sofa with Adam and read her Bible by kerosene lamplight, searching for something comforting to address her inner turmoil. Breeze occupied a recliner in the corner, Kenneth and Eric stretched out on the floor, and Julia and Dave curled up together on the love seat.

"Hey, here's a passage for us today," Tory called out, as a chapter in Psalms seemed to leap out and capture her attention. "Anybody want to hear it?"

"Yes!" Breeze rocked gently forward and back in the recliner, hugging a stuffed moose that Julia kept in the living room for just such a purpose. Kenneth and Eric both nodded eagerly.

Dave and Julia smiled at her. "Go ahead," Julia said.

Tory cleared her throat. "It's in Psalm 34:4-8. 'I prayed to the Lord and He answered me. He delivered me from all my fears. Those who look to Him are radiant, and they never have to cover their faces in shame. The poor man who is writing this cried for help; the Lord heard him and saved him out of every trouble. The angels of the Lord encamp around those who reverence Him and deliver them. Taste and find out for yourself how good God is. Happy is the man who takes refuge in the Lord.' "*

"That's a good one," Dave said. "It certainly applies to us." He turned to Breeze. "We're really glad you're here with us at Border Mountain, Breeze. We hope this will be a refuge as you sort out with God what you need to do to heal inside. Sometimes outward threats like wild animals can be small potatoes compared to the threat from our inside wounds."

Breeze nodded, tears welling up in her eyes. "I know," she whispered. "I'm finding that out." She held up the sprig of lupine she had picked in the logged over clearing. "But I found this promise in the berry meadow today. It was God's voice to me as surely as if He were standing right beside me and talking right out loud. He's going to make my life beautiful, even in the middle of destruction. And I'm going to let Him do it."

---

* The Clear Word

CHAPTER EIGHT

The warm days of late summer passed quickly. Adam and Dave kept busy every day except Sabbath, when they all attended a little A-frame church in the town 28 miles from Border Mountain. Tory breathed a sigh of relief when the sun set every Friday afternoon, for she knew that she could look forward to 24 hours of deeper connection with God, honoring Him as the Creator of everything she loved so much about the north country. She also loved the down-to-earth, practical sermons that Pastor Mark preached each week, and the people in the small congregation were like a family—warm and caring and welcoming to the newcomers.

On weekdays, Adam and Dave worked the horses from early morning until the first stars of twilight blinked on. Kenneth and Eric helped too, in between classes with Julia. Tory tried to ignore her feelings of loss at Adam's long hours away from her. She knew they were in a race against time, for the entire supply of wood for the long, cold winter must be stacked in the woodshed before snowfall, and Kenneth and Eric would soon be returning to college in another state, leaving Adam and Dave to complete the task alone. Saskatoon and Knick-knick were in their element, lifting their feathered feet high with every step and arching their necks proudly as they pulled the heavy tamarack and fir logs from the forest.

Tory and Breeze kept busy, too, when Breeze was not in class with Kenneth and Eric or spending quiet time with her journal and Bible. Together they picked berries, canned elderberry and saskatoon syrup, and ground fresh wheat berries into flour for homemade bread. They found an old apple tree loaded with early apples in an abandoned orchard not far from the lodge and picked several boxes full for applesauce.

Tory loved the smell of the cooked apples as she pushed them through the applesauce maker. The cores and peelings dropped out the back of the machine, and the rich, golden applesauce poured out the front into a huge stainless steel pot. The apples were so sweet she didn't need to add any sugar, but a dash of cinnamon and nutmeg gave the sauce a pungent spicy smell.

Breeze pulled the clean, hot canning jars from the oven and scooped the steaming applesauce into each jar, sealing it with a rubber-lined lid. Then she dropped the jars one by one into the canning kettle full of water that bubbled on the stove. She saved a kettle full of applesauce and placed it on the wood stove to cook down for several days into apple butter.

By late afternoon one hot August day, thirty-five jars of applesauce stood in a row on the countertop. Julia smiled at Tory and Breeze, clearly pleased with their accomplishment.

"They're beautiful, aren't they?" Tory said, pulling off her bright-red apron over her head. "I feel like they're my children, I'm so proud of them."

Breeze laughed. "I feel that way too. But I hope I change my mind before it's time to eat one of them."

The sound of horse's hooves clomping up the driveway drew Tory to the window. Adam trotted behind the horses, careful to sidestep the massive log the horses were pulling. Sweat lathered Saskatoon and Knick-knick's chests, and their nostrils flared as they battled the heavy log.

"Whoa there, boys," Adam called out. The Belgians pranced to a stop. Adam unhooked the log and maneuvered the horses around the growing log pile to the hitching post outside their corral. He clipped their lead ropes onto their halters, tethering them to the hitching rail while he stripped off their harnesses piece by piece. Kenneth and Eric, who were cutting and stacking wood into the shed beside the garage, looked up from their work and waved a greeting to Tory as she hurried outside to help Adam with the heavy collars.

"You're quitting early today," she said, planting a quick kiss on the back of Adam's neck. "Not that I mind, of course. What's up?" She pulled several handfuls of apple peeling from her pocket and fed them to Saskatoon and Knick-knick.

"Dave and I decided everyone had earned a treat today." Adam grinned at Tory. "How does a swim in the lake sound to you? We may not have many more of these warm afternoons. We'd best take advantage of this one."

"Woo-hoo," Tory whooped. "It sounds perfect. Let me go tell the others." She ran for the lodge just as Breeze came out the door to see what the commotion was all about. Eric and Kenneth dropped their axes and headed for the lodge to change. Within minutes, Tory and Breeze stood with Julia, Kenneth, and Eric, swimming suits on and towels draped around their necks, waiting for Adam to finish with the horses.

By the time the horses were cooled down, brushed, and watered, Dave had returned from the hillside where he had been scoping out standing dead tamarack to cut. He quickly changed into his swimming suit.

"All aboard," he called as he slid into the driver's seat of the lodge pickup truck. Tory, Adam, Breeze, Kenneth, and Eric climbed into the back of the truck and found comfortable seats on the wheel wells and sides of the pickup bed.

Adam winked at Tory. "Doesn't this remind you of riding in the back of the pickup in Honduras?"

Tory nodded and smiled at Adam. She glanced at Breeze and noticed that she was studying them, a look of pain in her soft hazel eyes. As soon as she saw Tory watching her, she looked quickly away.

Tory felt the old insecurity well up inside of her and for a moment she couldn't breathe. She wondered if Adam had seen Breeze's expression and if he wished he could talk to her and comfort her. Breeze was certainly beautiful in her sleek black swimming suit. Tory felt herself becoming smaller and smaller inside. *Help Father,* she prayed. *What is happening to me? This hurts too much.*

The lake looked inviting in the gathering shadows of early evening. The osprey that Tory and Adam had seen fighting the eagle when they first arrived, still sat perched in her nest at the west end of the lake. The babies were gone.

"I think we're disturbing her evening fishing," Julia said, pointing up to the nest. "It must be tough to try to coexist with humans."

Adam balanced himself on a protruding root at the water's edge. "Sorry, Mr. Osprey," he murmured, "but I'm going swimming." With that, he dived into the water, hardly leaving a ripple on the surface. Tory forced herself to set aside her painful thoughts for the moment, making a mental note to talk to Julia about them later.

"How's the water?" Tory shouted as Adam finally surfaced.

"Great!" Adam called back and disappeared under the water again.

Tory made her way carefully down the path to the root he had used as his diving board. She tossed her towel on the bank as she edged her way out. Holding her breath, she dived in.

As soon as she hit the water, an icy chill gripped her. She swam underwater for a few feet, then broke to the surface. "Adam Hartman," she shrieked. "This water is *freezing!"*

Adam paddled his way to the bank and pulled himself up onto the protruding root. He sat with his feet dangling in the water, laughing heartily as Tory swam back to the water's edge.

Kenneth and Eric dived right into the lake, but Dave and Julia waded in slowly, shivering as they made their way deeper and deeper. "I don't think this way is any easier," Julia called to Tory. "It still freezes every bone in your body." She dunked quickly under, then started swimming circles around Dave.

"Br-r-r," said Dave, shaking his head. "This is more like torture than fun, isn't it?"

The osprey left her perch in the snag and circled around the lake, screeching her objection to the intruders in her fishing hole. Dave dove quickly under the water, swam a short distance out into the lake, then turned around and swam back.

"OK. That's enough for me," he said, his lips blue with cold as he pulled himself out of the water.

"Me, too." Tory waded into the shallow water and

reached for the towel she had hung on the extending root.

"You folks aren't used to our Idaho snowmelt lakes, are you?" The strange voice behind her startled Tory. She looked up to see a middle-aged man in a red and green checked flannel shirt and a full, black beard watching them from the fishing dock. Although it was still summer, he wore a wool felt hat pulled down low over his face. A pair of coonhounds tugged at their leashes, held tightly in his left hand, while he puffed on an old-fashioned bowl pipe with his right.

The man squatted down on his haunches, a bemused expression on his face as one by one the whole group scurried out of the icy water and stood on the bank, shivering. Dave wrapped his towel around his waist and picked his way barefoot along the short trail to the dock.

"I'm Dave Zielinski," he said, stretching out his hand to shake with the stranger. "I don't believe I've had the pleasure of meeting you, sir." He motioned toward the group on the bank. "And that is Adam and Tory, our assistants; Julia, my wife; and Breeze, Kenneth, and Eric, three of our clients at Border Mountain."

The man grunted, set his pipe down on the dock, and grasped Dave's hand in a hearty handshake. "Name's John," he said. "I'm your nearest neighbor."

"So *you're* John," Dave exclaimed, letting the hounds sniff his hand in greeting. "I've been hoping to meet you ever since we opened the retreat center last spring."

"I live by myself," John said, gruffly. "I don't have a phone and I don't want one. I get out and see people if and when I need to." His expression softened as he looked over at the group. "I've seen you and the young man working those big horses of yours," he said, a note of respect in his voice. "I love animals. I'd like to come over and watch them work sometime if you don't mind."

Dave grinned. "Sure! We'd love to have you. Come anytime."

John shook hands with Dave again, then waved to the rest of the group. He spoke a stern word to the dogs and headed up the hill to the parking lot.

Tory watched in awe as John loaded the dogs into a brand new, full-sized, four-wheel-drive pickup truck. "That just doesn't seem like the truck a hermit would drive," she whispered to Adam.

"And just what kind of rig do you think he should be in?" Adam whispered back, a teasing tone in his voice.

Tory felt her face flush with embarrassment as she realized she was judging John and placing him in a pre-determined category in her mind. "Oops," she said softly. "No one deserves to be pigeon-holed like that. I was wrong to do it."

Adam slipped his arm around Tory's waist and pulled her close to him. "Do you know what I love most about you, Tory Hartman?"

"No, what?"

"That you listen when God tries to tell you something. I love that." He kissed her softly on the lips. Tory gulped. She wondered how Adam would feel if she told him what she'd been thinking about him and Breeze.

"Hey, you two. No PDA's." As if on cue, Breeze smacked Tory on the back of the head with her towel.

Just then, John reappeared at the edge of the parking lot. "Have you folks heard any mountain lions lately?" he asked, rubbing his black beard with a rough hand.

"Yes, as a matter of fact, we have," Julia replied. "The girls heard one several weeks ago. They were taking a walk and it screamed from the woods close by where they were."

John shook his head, his intense, coal-black eyes reflecting deep concern. "Be careful. Them critters get plumb nasty when they get hungry, and you know how bad last winter was. Why, I saw one kill a deer right in my side yard last February. Ate it there, too, right under the dog's noses. They pitched such a fit, I was sure it would scare the varmint away, but it didn't. That devil cat just kept right on a'eaten and snarlin' at the dogs like he had every right in the world to be in our yard."

Tory shivered, remembering the chilling scream she had heard in the woods. What kind of ferocious animal could make a sound like that? What if it came into the lodge yard even with Kodiak and Sardidi there? What if it got hungry enough to attack one of the horses, or worse yet . . . one of the *humans*. She felt herself falling into a vortex of fear.

Help me, Father, she prayed in desperation. *I know I can trust You. I choose to give this fear spin to You.*

She reached out and touched one of the massive pines that lined the trail to ground herself. A sense of peace flowed through her as she pictured herself being carried on God's broad shoulders. She took a deep breath and focused on the ways God had protected them in Honduras.

Adam touched Tory's hand. "Are you all right?" he whispered. "You seem like you're so far away. Is John's story scaring you?"

Tory shook her head. "It's OK. I'll tell you later."

That evening, as the group gathered in the living room to talk about their experiences during the day, Tory shared with the others her reaction to John and his mountain lion story. "I don't know what it is about that animal that sends me into such a panic," she said, leaning on Adam's shoulder and hugging the stuffed moose close to her chest. "Whatever it is, I learned something important today."

She paused and looked around at the group. A deep sense of safety and security washed over her like a warm, summer rain. Somehow, being able to speak honestly to this accepting and loving group healed a place in her that she hadn't even known was wounded.

"I was *so* panic stricken when John started talking about the mountain lion. Ordinarily, I'd be embarrassed about that and try to hide it, even from God." She propped the moose up at the end of the sofa and lifted up her arms. "Instead I held it up to Him, just as it was and asked Him to help me. Then I *chose* to move into relationship with Him by remembering what He's done in the past to help me, and to thank Him for those things."

Breeze leaned forward, studying Tory's face with keen interest. "And what happened then?" she urged.

"The fear spin stopped. Over. Gone." Tory felt tears welling up in her eyes and spilling down her cheeks. "It was amazing. A miracle."

Breeze let out a deep breath. "That's what I need to do," she said softly. "I think I've been spending a lot of my life in one big fear spin, especially since Brian and I got married. It's time it stopped."

Julia moved to Breeze's side and wrapped her arms around her. "We'll be praying for you, Breeze," she said. "You aren't alone anymore."

"I know," Breeze whispered. "I know."

CHAPTER NINE

By the third week in September a heavy cloud cover crept in over the valley, drenching every twig and leaf in a sodden mist. Kenneth and Eric had returned to college the week before. Tory already missed their friendly smiles and encouraging, helpful attitudes.

A herd of elk wandered into the clearing and munched on clumps of withered meadow grass. Tory held her breath as she watched them through the living room window with a pair of binoculars, careful not to make any sudden movements.

"Oh, don't be frightened, pretty ones," she whispered. "Stay and let me watch you for awhile." She knew Kodiak and Sardidi were sleeping away the rainy day in the snug, cozy wood shed. They would be little threat to these gentle visitors to the valley.

Breeze appeared at her side, her suitcases in hand. "What are you looking at?" she asked, peering out into the mist.

"Wapiti," Tory said, pointing to the little herd moving cautiously toward the beaver pond. "That's the Native American word for 'elk.'" It means 'ghost of the forest.'"

Breeze sighed. "I wish I could stay with you guys all winter. I'm going to miss seeing all the animals." She piled her suitcases by the door and plopped down on the couch. "I know I have to go back and put the information I've learned into practice, though. Every time I've asked God what to do lately, He's made it clear that I'm to go back to Brian."

"What about the abuse?" Tory asked, feeling a stab of concern for her friend. "Are you sure he won't hit you again?"

Hugging the stuffed moose close, Breeze shook her head. "No," she said in a small voice. "I don't know for sure that he won't. What I do know now is that I won't allow it to happen to me. I will set boundaries with him like Dave and Julia taught me and if he starts to get angry and abuse me, I have a safety plan in place."

She sat up straight, strength filling her eyes. "We'll both be seeing a counselor, individually and together. I learned all about the abuse cycle from Julia. If Brian even *starts* into the cycle by beginning to verbally abuse me, I have a place to go to be safe. We've talked about this a lot on the phone, and he knows that the old marriage is over. We either set new rules and begin a new marriage based on mutual respect or our relationship is over."

Tory set the binoculars down and moved close to her friend's side. "You know you can call us anytime, don't you?"

"Yes, I know." Breeze attempted a lop-sided smile. She sat quietly for a moment, then spoke in a faraway tone. "Many years ago, when we found out that my little sister was blind, I thought that nothing worse could happen in life. It was so hard to see her struggle to do the simplest tasks. I vowed that I would do anything I could to protect her from pain. I felt responsible for her."

Tory nodded. "I remember you telling me about that at Cool Springs Camp the year we worked there together."

Breeze stood up and walked to the wood stove,

where a fire crackled cozily. She backed up to the stove, standing as close as she could without burning her legs. "I was wrong to make that decision," she said, solemnly. "I meant well, but it was a vow I couldn't possibly keep."

She ran a hand through her short, black hair and shook her head as if trying to shake off the memories of the past. "Tory, I think I transferred that vow to Brian."

Tory raised her eyebrows in a questioning look, but Breeze hardly seemed to notice. She plunged on with her story, clearly eager to take the opportunity to speak the truth about the things she had been holding deep inside for so long.

"Brian's problems are not my fault," she continued. "His parents shamed him a lot and he got *hard* spankings every day. It's like they took out their own pain on him. What I've learned here at Border Mountain is that I can't fix that for him. I can only work on me. I actually made things worse by taking the blame when he tried to hang it on me."

Breeze walked back to the window and stood quietly for awhile, watching as the cow elk nudged her leggy calf into the path that led to the beaver pond. "When I talked to him on the phone last night he took responsibility for his own behavior. He said he's been going to counseling this whole time I was gone and that he feels he has a better understanding of his anger problem. I know it's rare for a batterer to ever change, but I feel that God can work a miracle in his life if he's willing to let it happen. I have to give it a chance."

Tory sat quietly, listening, trying to focus on what Breeze was saying, but her mind kept wandering back to the summers she spent so close to Brian at Cool Springs Camp. She pictured his broad, tanned back as he rode Bullet down the trail to the dark, murky Santa Fe River and his mischievous smile as he played tricks on the campers.

Brian, you deserve a chance to heal, she thought. *It'll be a long, hard road for both of you, but I know you'll make it.*

Just then Julia came down from one of the guest-rooms that she had been preparing for a new client. She smiled at the girls. "Looks like you're all ready to go, Breeze," she said, holding out a stack of books to her. "Don't forget these. They'll help you keep your perspective when you get home."

Tory noticed that two of the books were about boundaries and relationships. One was titled *Belonging* by Ron and Nancy Rocky,* the other was called *Understanding Intimate Violence,* by Barbara Couden.[†] She made a mental note to get a copy of each of them for herself.

Adam and Dave trooped in from the woodshed just as Breeze picked up her bags to take them to her van. They shook the sawdust from their clothes and each took a bag from her.

"We'll carry these," Adam insisted. "It's really soggy out there. Just concentrate on missing the worst mud puddles."

Dave held up his hand as Adam turned to carry one of the suitcases out the door. "Wait," he said. "Let's pray together before Breeze leaves."

The little group stood in a circle and held hands as Dave led them in a prayer of protection for Breeze, both on her journey home and on her journey toward healing with Brian. When the prayer was over, Breeze hugged each of them, tears welling up in her eyes.

"I'll never forget my time here," she said, giving

Tory a bear hug. "Write me, OK?"

"I will."

And with that she was gone. Tory watched as her van made its way down the muddy rutted road and disappeared into the forest. *Go with her, Father,* she prayed. *She's going to need You a lot these next few months.*

"Hey, who's up for an afternoon of trail clearing?" Dave held up a small chainsaw, a long handled branch pruner, and some other hand tools. "We have a limited time before snowfall to clear the Wild Horse Trail on the other side of the valley so we can use it in the winter for snowmobiles."

Julia shook her head as she glanced over Dave's shoulder at the dreary weather. "Not me, sir," she said. "I have an urgent batch of bread to bake."

"I'll go," Adam said, laughing.

"Me, too." Tory took one of the pruning tools from Dave and slipped into her rubber boots and raincoat.

The elk scattered as Dave, Adam, and Tory tromped their way across the yard and into the meadow, Kodiak and Sardidi close on their heels. As soon as the dogs saw the herd, they bolted across the meadow in hot pursuit. Almost as if by magic, the elk immediately disappeared into the surrounding forest.

"Ghosts of the forest," Tory whispered as she slogged along behind the men. "You came by your name honestly, *Wapiti.*"

They crossed the rushing creek at the edge of the meadow on an old wooden footbridge that creaked and groaned with every step. Tory jumped gingerly over, trying not to put too much of her weight on the questionable structure.

The swamp beyond the meadow lay in dark silence, absorbing the falling moisture into its murky depths.

With chainsaw tucked tightly under one arm, Dave led them across the swamp by leaping from root wad to root wad. Tory and Adam followed at a short distance.

Soon the swamp gave way to a dense wooded area with clusters of shaggy parasol and wood mushrooms dotting the loamy forest floor. Suddenly a road opened up before them. Fallen trees blocked the way every few hundred yards and young saplings encroached on its edges, but it was clearly a road.

"Welcome to Wild Horse Trail, the only highway through this valley back in the 1800s," Dave announced grandly. "We have the privilege of maintaining it for posterity's sake." He took a swipe at one of the saplings blocking the path, grinning at Adam and Tory. "Or at least for a good winter of snowmobiling."

Adam laughed. "Hey, whatever works," he said, grabbing the sapling that Dave cut down and dragging it into the woods at the edge of the road.

Tory glanced around and noticed that Kodiak and Sardidi had disappeared. She listened for Sardidi's high-pitched bark, but all she could hear was the soft pattering of the raindrops on the leaves around her. Even the squirrels were silent in the dankness of the damp forest.

Firing up the chainsaw, Dave began to cut a fallen tree into sections for Tory and Adam to lug to the edge of the trail. "We'll come back for these later," he shouted above the whine of the saw. "Let's just get them out of the way for now, and we'll burn them next year for firewood."

For hours they worked, Dave cutting the heavy branches and large logs and Tory and Adam clearing debris from the trail. They made slow but steady progress.

Tory noticed that they developed a rhythm as they

worked, almost like a dance. Cut, move, toss . . . cut, move, toss . . . Each maintained a position in the trail, Dave and Tory facing the swamp as they worked, and Adam facing down the trail.

Darkness gathered in the dim woods as the afternoon waned. "Just one more section," Dave called out over the sound of the saw. Tory bent down to pick up a handful of brush from the trail and felt the ground shake beneath her feet.

Puzzled, she stood straight, glancing at Dave to see if he'd cut down a large enough tree to vibrate the ground like that. Then she saw Adam's face. He stood, ashen faced in the trail, his eyes wide in astonishment.

"D-did you see *that?*" he gasped.

Tory wheeled around to look in the direction Adam pointed but saw nothing but an empty trail. A few seconds later, Kodiak and Sardidi raced down the path toward them, their tongues hanging out of their mouths.

Dave shut down the chainsaw and stood in the trail, a bewildered look on his face. "What is it, Adam?" he asked.

"It was a moose," Adam sputtered. "A *monstrous* moose. It came flying down the trail like it had been shot out of a cannon, headed straight for you, Dave." He shook his head in amazement. "I'm not sure he even saw you until he was almost on top of you. Then he made a 180-degree turn right between you and Tory and plowed into the woods over there. He couldn't have missed either one of you by more than a few inches."

Dave stared at Adam, struggling to comprehend what he was saying. He set the chainsaw down and bent over to examine the deep hoof prints in the soft dirt of the trail that led right to the place where he stood before abruptly veering off and disappearing into the woods.

Then he turned to Tory and burst into laughter. "And we never even *saw* him!"

Just then, the dogs returned, obviously abandoning their wild moose chase. They flopped down at Tory's feet, exhausted. She squatted down and took the dog's muzzles in her hands.

"Listen to me, you two," she scolded. "You're supposed to be helper dogs and protect us from the wild critters, not run us over with them." Sardidi rolled over and waved her paws in the air.

"I don't think she's too sorry," Adam said as he bent down to scratch Kodiak behind the ear. "I'll have to teach them not to chase everything that runs."

Dave looked doubtful. "Good luck," he said.

"Maybe we should build a kennel and keep them penned up," Adam suggested. "I hate to see them chasing all the animals."

Dave nodded. "Good idea." He picked up his chainsaw and started down the path toward home. "But let's think about it later. Right now I have an appointment with a loaf of fresh homemade bread."

---

* Pacific Press Publishing Association, Nampa, Idaho.
† Review and Herald Publishing Association, Hagerstown, Maryland.

CHAPTER TEN

The first soft flakes of snow fell four days before Thanksgiving. They fell silently and steadily all morning, blanketing the entire valley. Just before lunch, Tory donned a down coat and pulled a wool stocking cap over her ears. Then she headed out the door to feed Kodiak and Sardidi. She shivered as the icy air hit her cheeks. The outdoor thermometer hanging over the garage door registered 16 degrees.

Hearing the rattle of their food pans, Kodiak and Sardidi emerged from under a pile of straw in the kennel Dave and Adam had built for them. Spears of straw stuck out from their coats at crazy angles. Tory placed their food on a mat inside the kennel door and stood back to watch them eat.

"You both look like scarecrows," she said. "I'm sorry you have to stay caged up. It's *cold* out here."

She peered through the screen of falling snow to see if she could catch a glimpse of Adam and Dave and the horses. They had decided early that morning to try to pull in the last few logs to cut for firewood before the snow got too deep for the horses to get into the woods.

Julia stood at the kitchen sink cutting vegetables for stew as Tory scurried back into the kitchen, backing up to the crackling wood stove for warmth. She smiled at the older woman, enjoying the moment alone with her.

The more she got to know Julia, the better she liked

her. She loved the way Julia saw every occurrence in life as an opportunity and an adventure. Even chopping vegetables seemed fun with her.

"Do you mind if I talk to you about something?" Tory asked, feeling suddenly shy. Her heart pounded and her mouth felt dry as she realized she was about to share something with Julia that she'd never dared to speak of to anyone before.

Julia handed her a knife. "Of course not," she said, offering a handful of carrots for Tory to chop. "Talk away. I've been known to listen well at times."

Tory stared down at the carrots in her hands. "It's about Adam," she murmured. "Well, really more about me." Julia nodded supportively, encouraging Tory to go on.

"I get so, well, so *jealous* of him sometimes. Of the time he spends away from me, of how he looks at someone else, like Breeze when she was here. I don't like the way I feel and I can't seem to stop it." She sighed. "I just want to withdraw from him, but then I'm afraid he won't even care if I'm not there, that he'll be just as happy to be without me. He seems so content just to stay busy."

Julia stood quietly for a few moments methodically cutting a potato wedge into tiny cubes. When she spoke, she seemed to weigh her words carefully, as if trying to pick just the right ones to describe something very important.

"I know what you are talking about," she said softly. "I have the same problem with Dave. It took a lot of prayer and being willing to talk to other women about it before I could even begin to understand what was happening inside me. I call it the 'Michal syndrome' after King David's wife, Michal, in the Bible. Do you remember her story? She didn't like the fact that other women were praising David and he danced without his royal robes in the city."

Tory nodded. "I remember that story. If she felt like I did when Breeze was here, I feel sorry for her."

"I thought you'd relate," Julia said, laughing. "It really hurts to feel invisible like that. I found that it comes from having a dad that was gone a lot or turned away from his daughter for some reason when she was little. The daughter tries all her life to fill that 'daddy' space with someone else, but it never works. When her man turns his attention away, she feels like she disappears and the fear comes rolling in like a heavy fog."

Tory set her knife down on the counter and stared at Julia. "That's *exactly* how I feel. And my dad was in the service and gone a lot when I was growing up. It has seemed so silly that I've been afraid to tell Adam about it, but this makes sense."

"Maybe you can talk to him about it now," Julia suggested. "Speaking honestly and openly is one of the ways to break through the pain." She dropped a bowl full of chopped potatoes into the bubbling water on the stove. "And you hit on the most important way this past summer when you were frightened by John's story about the mountain lion. Do you remember?"

Tory shook her head, puzzled. "No. I don't."

"You told the rest of us that you had been swirling in a fear spin and made a choice to hold the whole thing up to God just as it was and ask Him to help you. You *chose* to move into relationship with Him by thanking Him for all the ways He's helped you in the past and by just talking to Him about how you were feeling. It broke the fear spin."

"I remember now," Tory whispered. "So you're

telling me that the Michal syndrome is a fear spin that God can help me with?"

Julia nodded. "That's what I'm saying. I'm living proof that it works. God is the only one that can fill that place of emptiness inside me anyway. Once I get out of my fear spin there may actually be some boundaries that need to be set. I can't work on those, though, if I'm all tied up in pain knots."

"Wow." Tory shook her head in amazement. "I'm glad I talked to you. I think I *can* explain this to Adam now. Maybe he won't think I'm crazy after all." She dumped her sliced carrots into the stewpot and wiped her hands on a kitchen towel.

Slipping back into her coat and hat, she peered out the window. "I'm going out to see if I can find the guys," she said. "I need some time to walk and think about what we've talked about. They said they'd be working on the mountainside just past the clear cut on the north road."

"All right," Julia said, smiling at Tory. "I'll put the cornbread in the oven. It should be just done when you all get back."

As Tory trudged up the snow-covered road, she looked around at the mountainsides. Even with a cap of snow weighting down every branch, it was clear that the surrounding color scheme had changed dramatically with the cold weather. Formerly green tamarack's bristled bright yellow and the maples were busily shedding the last of their red coats.

Tory heard the team before she saw them. The muffled clomping of heavy hooves on snow-packed ground echoed from the hillside where they were working. She caught her breath as she rounded the corner and saw Adam driving the team down a steep embankment, two huge logs chained to their harnesses. Adam waved at her and grinned broadly.

"Watch these guys work, Tory," he shouted. "They're awesome."

She sat on a stump where she had a bird's-eye view of the hillside, jamming her gloved hands deep into her pockets for added warmth. She could see her breath steaming in the frigid air.

Saskatoon and Knick-knick seemed to realize that they had an audience. They lifted their tails high and practically danced down the bank, pulling the logs smoothly along behind them. Adam unfastened the logs and reined the horses to the other side of the road where a log lay wedged between the embankment and a dense patch of forest that grew close to the road.

"We're going to try for this one," Adam called out. "It looks stuck pretty bad, but maybe we can budge it." He positioned the horses in front of the log and fastened the chain in place. "Come on, Sas. Get up there, Knick," he coaxed.

The Belgians leaned into the traces with all their might, the muscles bulging in their chests, but the log didn't move a centimeter. The horses stopped pulling and rested for a moment. Adam encouraged them forward. "Try it again, guys."

After another unsuccessful attempt, the horses stopped again, their nostrils flaring and their breath freezing in the air. Adam shook his head at Tory. "I think it's a 'no-go,'" he called.

Just then Saskatoon craned his neck around, looking for all the world as if he were sizing up the log and its position on the hillside. Then he turned, with Knick-knick following his lead, and plodded through the snow in the opposite direction. A shocked Adam dropped the reins and stood back, allowing the horses to move freely at will.

As the chain tightened on the log, the end raised up, loosening it from the surrounding dirt and rocks. As soon as it was clear that the log was loose, Saskatoon and Knick-knick moved back into position in front of the log and together pulled it free.

Tory jumped from her stump and ran toward the horses. Adam picked the reins back up and guided the horses, with the log in tow, to the growing pile at the base of the hillside.

"Wow!" Adam said as Tory reached his side. "Did you see that?"

"I did," Tory said, still amazed. She moved to Saskatoon's side and smoothed his sweaty coat. She noticed how thick it had become since the temperature had taken a nose dive. "This guy doesn't even need a human to help him log. He can figure it all out on his own."

Adam grinned. "He needs me to fasten the chains, though."

They heard a yell and looked up to see Dave waving his arms at them from high on the steep hillside. He had toppled a mammoth tamarack and cut it into 20-foot sections. He motioned for Adam to bring up the horses.

Once he had the horses fastened to the first log section, Adam clucked to the horses, urging them forward. They dug their massive hooves into the dirt, "bunny hopping" to gain momentum. The log section moved behind them, bouncing over the rough ground until they reached a place where the bank plunged steeply down to the left.

They turned to the right, along the rim of the bank, but the log section suddenly pitched sideways and rolled down the bank, snapping the heavy chain and sending it flying through the air. The log kept rolling until it hit a tree with a sickening thud.

Saskatoon and Knick-knick squealed in terror as the chain snapped and one piece of it cracked against their hind legs. They reared straight up in the air, then broke into a wild run, heading back toward the house. "Oh, no," Tory whispered, as she watched the heavy metal bar fastened to their harnesses flop and clang with every rock and root wad they ran over, only serving to terrify them further.

Dave dropped his saw and headed for the lodge at a dead run with Adam close at his heels. Tory followed them, almost afraid to see what condition the geldings would be in when they reached their corral. When she reached the yard, Saskatoon and Knick-knick stood trembling next to the log pile, blood flowing from several cuts on their legs.

Adam sprinted for the house and returned with a basin of soapy water and some soft rags for cleansing the wounds. Tory held both horses' reins while Adam cleaned out Saskatoon's cuts and Dave worked on Knick-knick.

Julia brought out a tin of antibiotic ointment and dabbed it onto the cuts as soon as they were cleaned. "I think these guys have earned a break," she said, giving Dave a meaningful look. "Don't you think we have enough firewood for the winter now? It seems too slippery for the horses to be working on the mountain."

Dave rubbed his beard and nodded. "You're right, Julia. We'll have to find something other than logging for these guys to do for exercise until the snow is over."

Later, after the horses were fed and watered, they all sat around the lunch table eating hearty vegetable soup with thick slabs of fresh, buttered cornbread. Dave filled Julia in on what happened on the hillside and how the horses had gotten so spooked.

"You guys didn't hear the best part of the story, though," Adam spoke up. "Before the chain snapped, *I* tried to get them to pull a big log out of the lower bank." He went on to tell the story of Saskatoon's appraisal of the situation and how he just dropped the reins and let the horses decide how to successfully pull the log free.

Julia shook her head in wonder. "These guys are so smart it's almost spooky," she said, passing a bowl of fresh salsa down to Dave. "Let's hope they don't figure out how to unlatch the gate. They may hitchhike to Texas for a job with better pay." She chuckled at her own joke.

"Oh, speaking of pay," Dave added. "We got a donation in the mail today for some food supplies. I paid tithe on it and what's left is just enough for groceries for Thanksgiving dinner."

He turned to Adam. "Would you and Tory be willing to go into town today for some groceries?" He looked out the window. "I think the weather should be OK if it doesn't get any worse than this."

Tory felt a rush of excitement as she changed clothes after lunch. It had been weeks since she'd been to town, and just the prospect of seeing new faces and different scenery gave her a lift. She could hear Adam and Dave laughing and joking with Julia as they washed the lunch dishes. She wondered how Julia had managed before she and Adam came, being all alone here at the lodge when Dave was out working.

Most of the winding dirt road from the lodge to the main highway sloped downhill. Tory held her breath as the tires spun in a few of the low spots, but all in all the little red pickup truck did a great job under Adam's expert hand. As they drove by the lake, they could see the osprey circling over the center of the lake where patches of open water still remained. A thin layer of dark ice covered much of the rest of the lake.

"They say the ice gets thick enough to ride a snowmobile over," Adam said, casting a longing look at the lake's surface. "We can surely snowshoe over it by Christmas."

In town, it seemed to be Christmastime already. Candy canes hung on the lampposts and Christmas decorations lined the shelves in the stores. "You'd think they'd have the decency to wait until after Thanksgiving to start Christmas," Adam muttered. He pushed the cart up and down the aisles while Tory scrutinized the grocery list Julia had given her.

As they rounded the end of one of the displays, they almost bumped into a man with a dark beard and a wool felt hat. Tory apologized, then looked closer.

"Aren't you John, our neighbor?" she asked.

The man tipped his hat to her. "Yes. It's me in the flesh," he said gallantly. "And you must be with the folks at Border Mountain."

"Yes, we are," Adam spoke up. "Adam Hartman, and this is my wife, Tory. It's good to see you again, John." He reached out to shake the man's hand. Tory nodded and smiled.

"I'm surprised to see you two out with such a storm brewing," John said, shaking his head. "Me, I'm headed home. I had to get some feed for my dogs, but I wouldn't be caught out after dark tonight for anything."

Tory opened her mouth to speak, but John disappeared around the end of the aisle as quickly as he had appeared.

"What do you think of that?" Adam said with a soft

whistle of surprise. "We've actually gotten to *speak* to John twice now!" He glanced at his watch. "We'd probably better hurry. If he's right about that storm, we need to get home while we still can."

CHAPTER
ELEVEN

Tiny, frozen pellets hit the windshield with increasing force as Adam inched the pickup along the snow-covered road. The wind howled and shook the truck, almost pushing it sideways in the road.

Tory sat quietly praying as Adam hunched over the steering wheel, straining to see the lines on the sides of the road. After what seemed an eternity, the sign for Robinson Lake appeared and they turned onto the campground road.

The wind shrieked in the tops of the tamaracks as they made the turn onto the gravel road to the lodge. The edges of the road disappeared in a swirling mass of whiteness. Adam laughed nervously.

"John was certainly right about this storm," he said, clearing the moisture from the inside of the windshield with a paper towel and squinting into the darkness.

The road grew steeper as they approached the first hill and the tires started to spin. Tory watched Adam's face grow pale as the truck fishtailed back and forth across the road, slipping on the icy grade. Soon it stopped completely.

Adam switched off the engine and stepped out of the truck to check the situation. Tory hopped out and joined him in the road. The tires had spun through the snow and ice and into the gravelly mud beneath. They were stuck.

"It's a good thing we have warm coats on," Tory said, pulling the hood of her jacket up over her head. "It looks like we're walking tonight."

Adam sighed. "It does look that way." He dug around under the seat in the truck and produced two flashlights. He handed one of them to Tory. "We'll need these. It's pretty dark out there."

Tory braced herself against the wind as she stepped out from beside the truck. The driving snow needled the skin on her face. She held one of her mittened hands up to her cheeks to try to protect them from the onslaught while she held the flashlight with the other. She noticed that Adam was doing the same thing.

Everything on the bleak, forsaken road looked different to Tory in the blizzard. Even the bridge across the creek took on a strange, ominous appearance as it loomed up in the darkness. Tory stayed just a little behind Adam so she could step into his footprints instead of continually breaking the crusted snow herself.

"Tory," she heard Adam call back to her over his shoulder. His voice sounded thin and far away even though he walked just a few steps ahead of her. "Let's have some prayer time."

Tory hurried to catch up with Adam and placed her mittened hand on his arm. He stopped quickly and she could sense him turning to face her. "I need to talk to you about something first," she said.

"What is it?" His face, even in the faint light of the flashlight, registered deep concern. She hesitated, not sure how to begin, then plunged ahead, leaving nothing out about her conversation with Julia.

Adam's mouth dropped open in surprise as Tory told him about the pain she'd felt when he and Breeze met. She felt more than saw his shoulders stiffen defensively. He started to turn away from her, then just sat down in the snow, his flashlight falling into the drift beside him.

"Are you telling me you don't trust me?" His voice sounded tight and far away.

Tory plopped down in the snow next to him. The trees overhead creaked and groaned in the wind. "No," she said. "It's not about you. It's about feelings that come up in me from a long time ago. I'm just beginning to learn about them. I just need to be honest with you and let you know where I am. I hope you'll understand and support me in this."

Adam nodded. "I hear you," he said, the edge gone from his voice. "I guess I was taking it personally." He stood up and brushed the snow from his jeans, then leaned over and kissed Tory. "I want to be supportive. Maybe Julia and Dave can help me learn how to do that."

Tory slipped her arm around Adam's waist and hugged him. "Thanks," she said. "I'm ready to hike and pray for people now."

For the next two hours they took turns calling out names of people to pray for. When they had lifted up the names of every family member and friend they could think of, they started praying for specific ministries they knew about. Then they prayed for all the clients that would come to Border Mountain and each of their family members. By the time they stumbled onto the porch of the lodge, Tory realized that not once on the whole three-mile hike against the roaring elements had she felt an ounce of fear.

Julia and Dave met them at the door, their brows furrowed with concern. "Are you guys all right?" Julia asked, drawing Tory to the wood stove and helping her out of her snow-caked coat and hat. "We've been praying for you ever since the storm hit. Did the truck make it up the hill?"

Adam shook his head. "No," he said. "Not even halfway. We walked the whole three miles."

"No wonder you look like snowmen," Dave said. "I haven't seen a storm like this in a long time. God was certainly walking with you out on that road."

Tory glanced at Adam and smiled. "Yes. He was."

Adam paused before taking his coat off. "You know, I think I'll peek at the horses before I get out of my duds, just to make sure they're faring OK in the storm." He turned to go back outside.

"Just a minute and I'll go with you," Dave said. "I checked them a couple hours ago, but I agree—it'll be good to know they're still doing fine." He grabbed a heavy, warm coat from the peg by the door and put it on. Shoving a stocking cap down on his head, he followed Adam outside.

In seconds, the two were back, alarm written all over their faces. "The horses are gone!" Dave exclaimed. "The gate was open and the hoofprints led out to the road."

Tory sank down on the couch. "Oh, no," she groaned. She thought of the speeding trucks with semi-trailers that barreled down the main road. If the horses made it that far, they would surely be killed in the storm.

She knew Adam was thinking the same thing and wouldn't rest until they knew the horses were safe, even though he was completely exhausted. She started to put on her coat to join them in the search, but Julia raised her hand.

"No, Tory," she said gently. "You and I need to stay here, inside where it's safe. We don't know what the men will encounter out there. We can't help them if we get lost out in the woods. We'll keep hot drinks ready and stay by the phone to call for help if necessary."

It seemed like hours later that the men returned, stamping the snow from their feet and peeling layers of snow-covered clothing in a pile by the roaring wood stove. Adam backed up to the stove and held his hands behind him to warm them.

"Well? Did you see any sign of them?" Julia asked Dave.

Dave shook his head soberly. "We saw where they turned aside on a logging road about a mile down. That road leads straight to the main highway. I'm really concerned that they may get out there and get hit, but there's nothing we can do. The snow is too deep to go after them in a vehicle and we searched everywhere on foot. They've completely alluded us."

"I wonder what scared them so that they'd run away like that," Tory mused. "Why would they leave their safe corral where they have shelter and food to take off into a storm?"

Adam cleared his throat. "I think I know why," he said quietly. "I saw mountain lion tracks in the snow near the corral. They had to be pretty fresh, or they would have been obliterated in this storm. The mountain lion was stalking the horses and spooked them enough that they broke the gate to get out."

Tory gasped. She thought of the story John told of the mountain lion eating a deer right in his front yard—in front of his dogs. She wondered if the mountain lion would attack one of the horses. Then another, more frightening thought came to her. *What if the mountain lion had followed Adam and Dave as they searched for the horses?*

As if he could read her thoughts, Adam moved to

Tory's side and put his arm around her. "Angels are bigger than mountain lions," he whispered in her ear.

Dave reached for Julia's hand. "Let's pray," he said, his voice clear and calm. "God knows where those horses are." He motioned for Tory and Adam to join him and they all held hands in a circle.

"Father," Dave prayed. "You saw the horses leave and You know the danger they are in. We've done all we can do in searching for them. We need a miracle. We're asking that you send angels to lead the horses back to us. In Jesus' name, Amen."

Julia poured cups of tea for everyone and passed around a huge bowl of freshly popped corn. The wind continued to howl around the eaves of the house, and spiky snowflakes spit against the windows with a fury.

Tory curled up on the couch and opened her Bible. *We need some encouragement right now, Father,* she prayed. *Could you give us something to hang onto?* She turned to the book of Isaiah, verses 1, 2, and 5.

"Here's a passage for us," she said, holding up the Bible. Everyone fell silent and listened. " 'Don't be afraid, I have redeemed you. I have named you. You are mine! When you walk through deep waters, I will be with you. When you pass through swollen rivers, they will not flow over you. When you walk through fire you will not be burned, neither will the flames harm you. . . . So don't be afraid. I am with you.' "

"I didn't hear anything about raging blizzards and lost horses in there, but I think we get the idea." Adam grinned at Tory and hugged her close to him. "I know the horses are in His hands."

Julia disappeared into the office and returned a few minutes later with a book in her hand. Tory caught a glimpse of the cover. It had a picture of an Indian riding on a war pony on the front.

"Anybody want to hear a great story?" Julia asked. "We can take turns reading. This one is one of my favorites."

Tory closed her eyes and leaned on Adam's shoulder as Julia's clear, soft voice rose and fell in a soothing rhythm. She loved stories about settlers and Indians on the frontier in centuries past. She'd often wished she'd been born in another era. Opening her eyes and looking around her in the lodge, she could almost imagine she *was* a pioneer woman in the 1800s. The soft flicker of the kerosene lamp danced on the thick log walls and the fire crackled in the stove. She closed her eyes again, letting the story take her away to another place and time.

Suddenly Adam sat bolt upright beside her. "What was that?"

"What?" Dave stood up and walked to the window. He stared out into the swirling darkness. The sound came again, a rhythmic thumping, like the pounding of horse's hooves galloping on snow.

Dave grabbed a flashlight and ran to the door. Heedless of the gusts of wind that blew snow into the kitchen, he threw it open and shined the flashlight out into the night. A familiar nicker sounded from the yard just outside the garage.

Tory, Adam, and Julia all raced for their coats and were outside in a flash. There in the area just in front of their corral, stood Saskatoon and Knick-knick, their chest's hot and sweaty from the exertion of their run. They all held hands again and knelt right there in the snow to thank God for bringing the horses back.

Dave snapped lead shanks onto each of their halters

and led the Belgians into the corral, securing the gate with a piece of rope. "I wonder what the angels used to lead them back," he said, a huge grin on his face. He walked over to Kodiak and Sardidi's kennel and opened the gate. "Here you go, guys," he said. "You won't be jailed anymore. We need you to do guard duty, even if you do get a little mixed up as to which animals you should chase and which you shouldn't."

Kodiak and Sardidi danced and leaped around Tory and Adam, overjoyed to be free again. Adam leaned over and patted each of the dogs. "Just keep that mountain lion scared away, OK?"

CHAPTER TWELVE

The valley looked like a frozen winter wonderland when Tory awoke the next morning and peeked out. Delicate frost designs swirled over the glass of the windowpane. Although the sun was already climbing in the southeastern sky, the outdoor thermometer hanging from a nail in a tree registered minus 10 degrees.

Tory pulled her robe tightly around her shoulders and shivered. She heard the stomping of hooves in the driveway and guessed that Adam and Dave were already at work with the horses. She dressed hurriedly, donning her warmest corduroys and a heavy sweater.

When she went to the sink to wash her face, no water came from the faucet. Puzzled, she turned the handle to the off position, then back on again. Still nothing. She ran a brush through her hair and braided it, then hurried downstairs to find Julia.

The tantalizing smell of grilling hash browns met her nose as she entered the kitchen. Julia sat on a stool at the counter, leafing through a cookbook. She looked up and smiled at Tory.

"Good morning," she said. "Ready for some breakfast?"

Tory backed up as close as she could get to the wood stove where the hash browns sizzled in a huge frying pan. "Yes, I certainly am," she said, inhaling deeply. "Anything I can do to help?"

"Well, we need oven toast if you want to make it, but everything else is pretty much done."

Tory nodded and moved over to the sink to wash her hands. When she turned on the faucet, nothing happened.

"Uh, Julia, I think we might have a problem here." She tried again. By this time, Julia was at her side, moving the faucet.

"Oh, no," Julia groaned. "This isn't good. The water line must be broken, and the holding tank just drained out. We have new clients coming in next week. We can't have anyone here if we have no water."

She opened the kitchen door and called Dave and Adam to breakfast. The men took off their boots in the hallway, then made a beeline for the wood stove to warm their hands.

"It's *cold* out there." Dave rubbed his hands together over the hot air rising from the stove. Tory noticed a bright pink glow in Adam's cheeks from the biting cold. He noticed her watching him and hurried over to give her a good morning kiss.

Tory cut the bread and arranged it on a baking pan to put in the oven for toast. She'd thought it an odd way to make toast when she and Adam first arrived, but now she liked it even better than toast made in a toaster.

Dave moved to the sink to wash for breakfast. He turned the faucet on and off just as Tory had, a puzzled look on his face. "Isn't there any water?" he asked Julia.

Julia shook her head. "It appears not," she said, a weary tone in her voice. "I hope it doesn't mean what I think it means." She brightened and smiled at Tory and Adam. "But breakfast is ready. Let's eat a good meal, then deal with it."

After a hearty breakfast of hash browns, toast and country gravy, and scrambled eggs, Dave and Adam disappeared outside to check the water line. In less than 30 minutes they were back.

Dave shook his head. "I don't know how it happened," he said. "The water line is frozen solid. The only thing I can figure out is that the overflow pipe got clogged, and the water movement stopped long enough for ice to form." He sat down on a stool at the counter and slumped over, his head in his hands. Julia moved to his side, slipping an arm around his shoulders.

"What are the chances of thawing it out?" she asked hopefully.

Dave sat up and looked her straight in the eye. "None. Unless we have an early spring thaw." He sighed and stood up slowly. "We'll have to haul enough water from the pond to flush toilets and water the horses. We can boil and filter it for drinking and cooking."

"I'll call and cancel our clients for the winter," Julia said. Tory saw a panic flit across Julia's face, quickly followed by an expression of peaceful determination. Dave nodded in agreement, then turned to Adam and Tory.

"I guess with this turn of events, we'd better fill you in on how things stand. With no clients here this winter, we have no income, unless donations come in from various supporters. We will have no money to pay you." He stood up and put one huge hand on Adam's shoulder and the other on Tory's.

"I don't expect you to work for nothing," he continued. "If you choose to go, we understand, but we want you to know that we'd love to have you stay. There are ample food supplies for us to get through the winter no matter what money comes in."

Adam glanced at Tory. "Give us some time to talk about it and pray about it, OK?"

Julia and Dave busied themselves with cleaning up

the kitchen and taking stock of the pantry while Adam and Tory slipped into their heavy coats to take a walk and talk things over.

"What do you think?" Adam asked Tory as soon as they got outside, headed for the corral. Kodiak and Sardidi emerged from their warm bed under the hay in the barn and joined them, dancing in excited circles, begging for attention. Tory knelt down to greet them, letting Sardidi swipe her warm, wet tongue across her face.

"Do you mind spending a winter flat broke?" Adam studied Tory's face, trying to read her response. "You know how much savings we have. It's not much. I was counting on our being able to save a lot of what we made here this winter, working with Julia and Dave."

Tory looked up at Adam and then stood and brushed a snowflake from his eyebrow where it had fallen from a tree branch above them. She smiled. "I think we have a Father who 'owns the cattle on a thousand hills.' "*

"Does that mean you want to stay?"

Tory nodded. "Yes. We still need to pray about it and make sure it's what God wants, but I believe He sent us here for a reason. I feel that being here for Breeze was a big part of the reason, but I can't help sensing that there's more."

"I love you, Tory Hartman," Adam whispered, pulling her close. "I love the way you put God's will first in your decision making. I agree with you. It's what God has been impressing me with too. He wants us here. I don't know why, I just know."

A hoof stomped in the corral and a deep, throaty nicker pulled Tory's attention to the horses. Saskatoon stood next to the water tank, lifting his leg and pawing at the side. Knick-knick reached over the gate and gazed at Tory and Adam, a pleading look in his soft brown eyes.

"You guys are thirsty, aren't you?" Adam exclaimed as he peered into the empty tank. "We'd better get busy and find you some water."

Tory found several five-gallon buckets in the garage while Adam fired up one of the snowmobiles. "We'll be doing a lot of this for the next few months," he said, a boyish anticipation on his face. "We'd better figure out how to do it efficiently."

Tory laughed. "Right. You've been waiting for an excuse to use those snowmobiles. Now you have an ironclad one." She reached down and grabbed a handful of snow, packed it quickly into a snowball and threw it at him.

Adam ducked, laughing. "All right," he sputtered. "I admit it. Truce!" He jumped on the snowmobile, patting the seat behind him. "Let's get to work, partner."

A three-inch thick layer of ice covered the pond from the beaver dens all the way to the dam. "It's a good things the beavers have air holes," Tory mused. "I have a feeling this ice will get a lot thicker before winter is over."

Smashing a hole in the ice with a shovel, Adam filled the buckets one by one with the frigid water. Tory balanced the filled buckets around her on the running boards while Adam drove the snowmobile slowly up the hill to the corral.

Saskatoon danced nervously, nipping at Knick-knick in an effort to drive him away from the tank as Adam lugged the heavy buckets full of water to the gate. Tory swung the gate open and closed it again behind him. As soon as Adam poured the icy water into the tank, Saskatoon buried his nose in it, blowing bubbles at its strange odor, then drinking deeply until the whole five gallons was gone.

Adam emptied all four buckets into the tank, but it wasn't until he had polished off two bucketsful that Saskatoon allowed Knick-knick to drink. Tory patted Knick-knick's massive neck. "It's awful being the little guy, isn't it?" she soothed.

Just then Julia walked out of the lodge, a bright colored stocking cap pulled down over her ears and a fuzzy plush coat buttoned up under her chin. She waved a mittened hand as she approached.

"Good news," she said as she reached the corral. "We just got a call from Breeze. She says she and Brian are attending counseling together and are doing well. He's really working on his issues. She says he's learning to honor and support her instead of cutting her down and abusing her. Isn't that great?"

Tory reached out and hugged Julia, tears welling up in her eyes. "I'm so glad," she said. "I'm glad that she could learn some tools for dealing with the situation. What might have happened if she hadn't been able to come here?"

"I don't know." Julia shook her head sadly. "There certainly is a great need for places for people to find help like this. The only other one I know of is in Kentucky."

Glancing at Adam, Tory saw a strange mixture of determination and apprehension on his face. She raised her eyebrows at him questioningly, but he turned away quickly and started collecting the empty water buckets.

"Did you guys get a chance to think about whether you want to stay or not?" Julia asked.

Adam tossed the buckets over the gate. "Yes," he said firmly, winking at Tory. "We want to stay." Tory nodded in agreement.

Julia's face lit up as she smiled at both of them. "That's great. Dave will be very pleased. I'll go tell him."

As soon as Julia disappeared into the lodge, Tory turned to Adam. "What were you thinking when Julia was talking about the need for places like Border Mountain? You got such a funny look on your face."

Adam blushed. "So you saw that, huh?" He slipped out of the corral and fastened the gate behind him. "I was thinking that someday I want to do this very thing—you know, have a retreat center for teaching people how to heal from their hurts. It just scares me to think of the responsibility. And I wasn't sure how you'd feel about it."

"I can't think of a better way to help people," Tory said quietly. "It would take more education for both of us, but I'd be up for it. I can see what it has done for Breeze. We'll just have to hold it up to God and see what He says about it."

* See Psalm 50:10.

CHAPTER THIRTEEN

Christmas came and went, and still the water pipes remained frozen. Tory smiled as she remembered Christmas dinner. Julia had made a delicious roast out of Special K cereal, pecans, and cottage cheese. There had been cranberry sauce, piping hot biscuits with honey, fluffy mashed potatoes, and Dave's special "stuffing" with creamy pumpkin pies for dessert. Even the Belgians had a Christmas treat: a bucket of oats seasoned with sticky, black molasses. It had been a chore washing up all the dishes in pond water heated on the stove, but with everyone pitching in, the work was done quickly.

Now, in late February, Tory hardly noticed the inconvenience of lugging the heavy buckets of water into the house for bathing and dishes. It seemed a part of the routine and she accepted it without even thinking much about it. She emptied a few quarts of water into the canning kettle on the stove to heat for her bath, listening absentmindedly to the howl of the wind as it whipped down the valley.

"It sounds like another storm brewing," Adam said, stomping the wet snow from his feet as he came into the lodge from feeding the horses. "The wind is pretty fierce but not icy cold. We may get several inches of new snow before nightfall."

Tory opened the door to the stove and tossed another piece of wood on the fire. She turned to give

Adam a kiss but hesitated as she noticed a worried expression on his face. "Are you concerned about Dave and Julia?" she asked, helping him unwind the heavy wool scarf he'd tied around his neck.

Adam shook his head. "No. It's not that. They won't be back from their seminar until the day after tomorrow, and the storm will have blown over by then." He pulled off his boots and slipped his feet into a pair of fuzzy wool slippers.

"Want some tea?" Tory asked as she poured herself a cup of hot water from the teapot that sat on the back of the wood stove and plopped an orange spice herb teabag into the steaming liquid.

"No," Adam said, his voice tense. He started pacing the kitchen, glancing out the window every few seconds.

Tory set her tea on the counter and stood right in front of Adam. Taking his hands, she looked into his eyes. "Tell me what it is," she said. "If you're afraid you'll scare me, it upsets me more not to know."

Adam stared down at Tory's hands in his. "It's the mountain lion," he said in a low voice. "The tracks came right down to the corral this morning. The horses were huddled in the far corner, shaking from head to toe. They're terrified." He looked up at her, confusion in his deep, blue eyes. "I don't know what to do, how to protect them. The mountain lion doesn't seem to be afraid of the dogs at this point. With all the storms decreasing the deer population even more, he must be starving."

A knot formed in Tory's stomach. The sound of the wind outside took on a different tone. It was as if she could sense something ominous in the air, a dark presence waiting to attack. She shivered.

"See, I scared you." Adam frowned. "I didn't want that to happen."

Tory reached up and placed her hands on his cheeks, kissing him gently. "You, Adam Hartman, are not responsible for my feelings," she said. "It's OK. I wanted to know."

They busied themselves around the lodge for the rest of the day cleaning and seasoning Saskatoon and Knick-knick's harnesses, which Adam had hauled into the living room the night before. It was tedious work, rubbing the pungent oil into every crack and crevice of every piece of leather on the harnesses. Tory took a break mid-afternoon to prepare a batch of oatmeal raisin cookies.

"M-m-m." Adam sniffed the air as the cookies baked. "Nothing like oatmeal cookies to lift your spirits on a blustery winter day."

Suddenly, above the sound of the wind, a horse's sharp cry punctuated the air. Adam leaped to his feet and pulled his coat from the peg. He didn't bother to grab his hat or scarf, but jammed his feet into his boots as he headed for the door.

"I'll be right back," he called over his shoulder as he disappeared outside. "Don't eat all those cookies while I'm gone." The door slammed shut behind him.

Tory stood as if nailed to the floor, her mind racing. *Father, something is wrong. I can sense it. What do You want me to do?*

She slipped a hot mitt over her hand and pulled the cookies from the oven, then ran for her coat and gloves. The wind slammed into her face as she opened the door, almost taking her breath away.

Shuffling through the drifts of new snow, Tory lowered her head against the wind and headed straight for the corral. She could hear Saskatoon and Knick-knick squealing. Then she heard a raspy snarl and Adam's voice crying out. Her hands shook as she unlatched the gate to the corral and hurried inside.

Her heart froze in her chest. Saskatoon and Knickknick danced nervously back and forth along the far fence and Adam lay face down in the snow, blood pouring from a wound in his neck. A huge mountain lion, its yellow eyes glaring fiercely at her, crouched over Adam's still form.

O God, O God, what do I do? Tory gasped in horror, but her eyes never left the lion's cold gaze.

Make yourself look as big as possible, she heard a voice say somewhere inside her head. *Wave your arms.*

Tory gulped and raised her arms high in the air. Waving them wildly back and forth, she moved slowly toward the mountain lion, shouting, "Get out of here, you devil cat. Shoo. Shoo!"

The mountain lion snarled and lowered its head, its tail switching nervously back and forth. Then it turned and bounded away, clearing the corral fence in one smooth leap, and disappeared into the forest.

"Adam!" Tory shrieked, running toward the motionless figure in the snow. As she reached his side, she felt his wrist for a pulse. Hot tears of relief streamed down her face as she felt the faint tapping of his pulse against her fingers. She held her cheek down by his nose and felt the even puff of his breath.

"Thank God," Tory moaned. "You're alive."

The wound on the back of Adam's neck continued to bleed. Flinging her coat and outer sweater off, she pulled her cotton T-shirt over her head. Then she ripped the T-shirt into squares and used her scarf to hold the material over the wound.

"Call 911. Someone call 911," Tory whispered to herself. "That someone has to be *me.*"

She looked around wildly, acutely aware that the

mountain lion could return as soon as she left Adam's side. How could she get to the phone in the lodge without further endangering his life?

"Kodiak! Sardidi!" She screamed the dog's names until she was hoarse, but the wind blew against her and carried her voice in the opposite direction from where the dogs lay snuggled under the hay in the barn.

All at once she heard the faint sound of an engine and the muffled crunch of tires on new snow. The gate creaked open and suddenly John was bending over her, a worried expression on his bearded face.

"It looks like you need some help, missy," he said, his voice soft and even. "What happened?"

Fresh tears welled up in Tory's eyes as she told John about the mountain lion attack. He listened carefully, then stood straight. "There's no time to waste with a wound like that. I'll go call for the ambulance."

Within minutes, John was back, a pile of blankets in his arms. "They're on their way," he assured Tory. "Let's pile these on him to keep him warm while we wait. The paramedic said not to move him at all until they get here."

He tucked the blankets around Adam, avoiding the blood-soaked rags that Tory continued to hold firmly in place over the wound. She noticed with alarm that the bleeding continued, almost unaffected by the pressure she was putting on the wound.

Help us, Father, she prayed. *Please send the paramedics quickly.*

The snow continued to fall steadily, dancing in the wind gusts as if unaware of the seriousness of the situation in the corral. John looked around uneasily.

"I think I need to go down to the highway and meet the ambulance," he said. "This wet snow will make that steep road pretty treacherous. They may need my truck to get up here." He started to walk toward the gate, then turned back to Tory.

"You know, it's the oddest thing," he said softly. "I don't know what came over me this afternoon. I had no intention at all of going anywhere in this storm. Something just kept itching under my skin, saying, 'Get on over to those neighbors of yours.'" He shook his head in wonder. "You'd be in a frightful spot right now if I hadn't come. Somebody up there is a'lookin' out for you."

It seemed like hours before Tory heard John's truck pull into the lodge yard again. She heard voices, men's and women's, talking in hushed, measured tones. Then the gate swung open and a young woman in blue coveralls hurried into the corral carrying what looked like a large, plastic toolbox. She was followed by two older men in similar uniforms.

"Hi, I'm Darcy," the woman said, a kind look in her eyes. She reached out and grasped Tory's hand. Tory could almost feel the strength coming from the young woman's hand.

Darcy and the other two paramedics went right to work, checking Adam's blood pressure and pulse and inspecting the wound. When Darcy lifted the bandage, Tory saw fresh blood pulsing from the hole in Adam's neck. Her head began to spin and she felt a wave of nausea sweep over her.

The next thing she knew, Tory woke up in the back of John's truck as it inched slowly along the icy, snow-covered road. Thick sheets of snow pelted down as the paramedics held Adam tightly in the same position they'd found him in the snow, still wrapped in blankets. Tory knew they were concerned about spinal cord injury and wouldn't change his position until he had been X-rayed.

Adam opened his eyes and smiled weakly at Tory. He raised one hand and pointed up to the sky, then closed his eyes again.

"I think he's trying to tell you that God is taking care of things," Darcy said, reaching out to touch Tory's arm. "Are you feeling all right? You passed out cold back there. Right into a snow drift."

Tory reached back and felt the inside of her collar. "No wonder my neck is so cold," she said, pulling chunks of melting snow out of her hood. She blushed with embarrassment as she thought of fainting when it was Adam that needed attention. "I'm a nurse. I'm not supposed to faint at the sight of blood," she said sheepishly.

Darcy shook her head. "You don't have to be a nurse when it's your own loved one. You get to be a wife, and wives sometimes faint when they see their husbands injured."

Tory snuggled down in the blanket the men had wrapped her in, her hood protecting her face from the melting snow. She noticed that Darcy had positioned herself at Adam's head where she could not only continue the pressure on his wound, but use her own body to shield him from the driving snow and wind. Tory could see Darcy shivering, but she never uttered a word of complaint.

Father, sometimes You send people to give Your healing touch for You, don't You? she thought. *Darcy is definitely wearing Your skin today.*

CHAPTER
FOURTEEN

Peering out through the blinding snow, Tory could see a sheriff's vehicle waiting at the bottom of the mountain with the ambulance. As John pulled his pickup gently to a stop, two uniformed sheriff's deputies approached the back of the truck.

One of the men extended his hand and helped Tory climb out of the pickup bed. The other man assisted the paramedics in transferring Adam into the ambulance.

"Are you his wife?" the deputy asked Tory.

Tory nodded. "Yes, I am."

The deputy pointed to two men sitting in the back of his rig, rifles in their hands. Several long-eared hounds pressed their noses against the glass, eager to begin their hunt.

"These guys are going after that mountain lion," the deputy explained. "I just need your statement of what happened so we know for sure it was a big cat that attacked your husband. We'll track him until we find him. Anytime a mountain lion attacks a human, he has to be put down."

Tory told the story as simply as she could, all the while keeping an eye on the activity in the back of the ambulance. She felt a twinge of sadness for the doomed animal that lurked somewhere on the mountainside behind them. His hunger had driven him to do what he'd done. On the other hand, she felt a deep sense of relief that, with the mountain lion gone, Border Mountain would be a safer place.

As she climbed into the passenger seat in the front of the ambulance, Tory suddenly realized that it might be days before she returned. "The animals," she cried out. "The dogs and horses won't have anyone to feed them while we're gone."

John stepped up to her door. "I will feed and water your animals, Missy," he said, reaching out a hand to shake hers. "Don't you worry none 'bout them. You just concentrate on helping that man of yours, OK?"

Tears filled Tory's eyes. "How can I ever thank you, John? I could never repay you for what you've done for us."

John shook his head. "No need to thank me, young lady," he said kindly. "You'll have a chance to pass it on to another someday. That's all the thanks I need."

The ambulance, its siren blaring, raced as fast as its driver dared through the storm toward the little hospital. Tory clung to the door handle, her knuckles white. She could hear Adam moaning in the back as the paramedics started IV lines to try to replace the fluid in his body. She knew he had lost a lot of blood before the paramedics arrived, and she could hear them whispering something about not being able to get the bleeding stopped.

Father, I know Adam's life is in your hands, she prayed. *Please don't let him die. Our life together has just begun.*

As soon as they reached the hospital, nurses and doctors raced out through the emergency doors to grab Adam's stretcher and whisk him inside. Tory jumped out of the ambulance and followed the stretcher as far as she dared.

"You'll have to wait out here," one of the emergency room attendants told her as they wheeled Adam into a sterile-looking room with curtains all around it. The attendant pulled the curtain shut, leaving Tory standing outside. She stuffed her fist in her mouth to keep from screaming. Every cell in her body felt as if it were going to burst with the horrible feeling of separation from Adam when she felt he needed her the most.

Just then Pastor Mark appeared from behind the curtain. Tory ran to him, and he hugged her as she burst into tears, patting her back as if he were comforting a small child.

"I beat the ambulance here," he said. "One of the church members heard about the attack on their short-wave radio and called me. They're letting me stay in the room while they work on him." He held Tory out at arm's length and looked her straight in the eye. "He's in God's hands now. I'm praying constantly for him. And I'll listen carefully to what's happening and report back to you as often as I can."

Tory nodded mutely. She felt a wave of peace wash over her at the sound of Pastor Mark's comforting words. Once again, she had the overwhelming aware-ness that God was reaching out to her through another human being, letting her know through Pastor Mark's presence and assurance that He was with her.

True to his word, Pastor Mark slipped out of the room frequently and gave Tory reports. "I think they're shipping him to Spokane to the medical center there," he said on one trip to the waiting area. "The doctor will be out soon to talk with you about it."

He reached out and touched Tory's shoulder. "Just before they put the breathing tube in his throat, they asked him if he had anything to say." Pastor Mark's voice caught. "He said, 'I love the Lord.' He's ready for whatever happens."

Tory nodded, her throat too tight to speak. Just then the doctor—a kind-looking man with short dark hair and intense brown eyes—appeared. He pulled Tory into a small waiting room to talk with her.

"It's been nip and tuck," he said soberly. "We almost lost him when we couldn't get the bleeding stopped. He's lost a tremendous amount of blood. With your permission, we'd like to send him by emergency flight to the city."

"Whatever you need to do, Doctor," Tory whispered, her lips trembling as she spoke. "Is he going to live? Will he be paralyzed?"

The doctor shook his head. "It's too soon to tell." He patted her on the arm. "We're doing everything we can. The rest is in God's hands."

After the doctor left, Tory paced the larger waiting area. She felt the panic rising up inside her, like some giant hand squeezing her chest and threatening to cut off her breath. She walked over to a painting hanging on the wall. It was an ocean scene with crashing waves and wheeling seagulls. Standing as close to the painting as she could, she focused her vision on one wave in the picture. Then she narrowed her view until all she could see was the rich blue of the underside of the wave.

"That is blue," she said simply, pointing to the spot on the canvas. "Blue." She forced her mind to concentrate just on the color. *Thank You, Father, for the color blue.* The overwhelming feeling subsided and Tory took a deep breath. *And thank You that I can leave this whole nightmare in Your hands and trust You for the outcome.*

Just then Pastor Mark appeared in the doorway.

"They're taking him by ambulance to the airport. Want to ride in my car with me?"

Pastor Mark and Tory followed closely behind the ambulance with its wailing siren and brightly flashing lights. The wind continued to blow, sending snowflakes skittering across the road in front of them. Tory bit her lip as she studied the angry sky. *How will the emergency flight pilot get through this storm? Will he be able to see the runway lights of the tiny airport?*

When they reached the airport, Pastor Mark pulled his car up beside the ambulance. Tory jumped out of the car just as the crew opened the back doors to remove Adam's stretcher. She gasped as she caught sight of Adam, lying pale and deathly still on the gurney. A paramedic manually pumped air into a breathing tube protruding from his mouth. She reached for his hand, carefully avoiding the IV lines. It felt cool, and his fingertips looked blue. She felt no response to her touch.

A tall, serious-looking young man accompanied by two women in surgical scrubs under heavy winter coats approached the ambulance. Pastor Mark's face lit up as he recognized the man. "Kile, what are you doing here?" he exclaimed, rushing forward to hug his old friend. "I haven't seen you since college."

"I'm the pilot for this emergency flight," the young man replied. "And what a flight it's been! They told us we couldn't make it because of the storm, but we prayed and just as we were running low on fuel and thought we'd have to turn back, a hole opened up in the clouds and we were able to land. So here we are."

He reached out his hand to Tory. "I'm Kile," he said, grasping her hand. "Is this your husband we're transporting?"

Tory nodded, a lump rising in her throat.

"I'm sorry we won't have room for you to ride on the flight, but we'll meet you at the hospital," he said, still shaking her hand. "We'll take good care of him."

"She can ride with me. I'm driving," Pastor Mark said. He reached out to shake hands with Kile. "Thanks for being willing to risk your life like this. I know God sent you."

Kile tipped his flight cap and grinned as he turned to his plane. "Don't mention it," he called over his shoulder. "You'd have done the same."

How many heroes do you have in this world, Father? Tory mused, as she watched Kile walk away. *Dave and Julia, sacrificing their lives to help hurting people; John, listening to Your direction and going out of his way on a stormy afternoon; Pastor Mark, willing to stand by and support and pray through the long hours of waiting; Kile, risking his life in a small plane through a terrible storm; the doctors and nurses and paramedics and deputy sheriff. Thank You, Father. Thank You for all of them.*

CHAPTER FIFTEEN

A loud, insistent alarm sounded somewhere far away. *Why doesn't someone turn that annoying thing off,* Tory thought. She felt something cold on her cheek and slowly opened her eyes. The alarm continued, louder and more insistent, until she realized that it came from the IV machine right next to Adam's hospital bed.

She sat up and rubbed her cheek, suddenly aware that the cold thing her face had been lying on was a clipboard. Scribbled notes covered the paper it held. She looked up quickly to see Adam watching her, a smile playing at the corners of his mouth. The breathing tube was still in place, now attached to a sucking, hissing machine that Tory recognized as a ventilator.

Adam motioned for the clipboard and pencil. Tory, grinning wildly, her heart pounding, handed it to him.

"You fell asleep on me," Adam scribbled on the paper.

"I didn't even realize it," Tory sobbed, putting her arms around Adam the best she could while avoiding the spiderweb of tubes that surrounded him. "I didn't know you were awake!" She touched his cheek gently. "I love you. I'm so glad to have a chance to tell you how much."

Adam nodded, tears sparkling in his eyes. "I love you, too," he wrote. He looked deep into Tory's eyes then back to the clipboard. "God spared my life," he wrote, in a firm, decisive hand. "He has something special He wants you and me to do."

Tory took Adam's hand, tracing the pattern of his fingers with hers, tears dropping on the crisp white linens on the hospital bed. She looked up at him and smiled. "I know," she said. "He's been telling me the same thing. Everything we've been through is for a reason."

Just then, a distinguished looking, gray-haired gentleman in a long, white lab coat walked into the room. Tory stood quickly.

"Ah. I see that you're awake now, and your lovely wife is here with you," the man said. He extended his hand to Adam and then to Tory. "Allow me to introduce myself, although you and I have already met, Adam. You just don't remember it. I'm Dr. Wheeling, the surgeon who worked on you last night."

Adam reached for the clipboard and scrawled, "Thank you for taking care of me."

Dr. Wheeling shook his head. "Someone else was taking care of you, young man," he said solemnly, pointing up. "I just helped. You should have been a dead man with the injury you sustained. The mountain lion's tooth clipped one of your arteries—that's why you bled so much. But it came so close to your spinal cord, you should at least be paralyzed." He smiled as he patted Adam's arm. "You'll have a full recovery, thankfully. You should be off this machine soon and be able to go home by the end of the week."

For the next several days, nurses and other medical staff from all over the building poked their heads into the room to see "the miracle boy" they had heard so much about. As Tory helped one of the nurses bathe Adam, she was horrified to see how thin he was. She already knew his face looked sunken, but she was unprepared for how shockingly skinny his body looked.

"It's because he lost so much blood," the nurse whispered to her in the hallway after the bath was finished. "He'll gain it back. Wait and see."

Sure enough, the very day the breathing tube was removed, Adam ate an entire tray of food, gulping down the scrambled eggs, soup, and gelatin dessert as though they were gourmet fare.

"I haven't forgotten my oatmeal raisin cookies," Adam said, his voice still hoarse from having the tube in his throat. "Did you save them for me?"

Tory stared at him. "You've got to be kidding me. I haven't even thought about those cookies." She gulped. "I'm not even sure I took them out of the oven."

"You took them out," a voice spoke from the doorway. Tory turned to see Julia standing there with Dave close behind her. "And I saved your cookies for you." She grinned at Adam.

Dave strode to the bedside and enveloped Adam in a huge bear hug. "You scared us spitless," he said, his voice husky. "Thank God you're all right. We came as soon as we heard. John did a great job with the animals. Saskatoon and Knick-knick are fine. So are Sardidi and Kodiak." He paused, then continued in a sad voice. "The hunters found the mountain lion in a cave on one of the cliffs behind the lodge. He won't be threatening us anymore. They said he was pathetically thin and probably would have died before the winter was over anyway. He was sick and desperate for food or he would never have attacked a human."

Adam hung his head. When he looked up, pain filled his eyes. "I'm sorry the mountain lion had to die," he said. "I know he acted out of his own distress. I've forgiven him for hurting me."

The whole valley seemed to be celebrating with Tory on the day that they brought Adam back to Border Mountain from the hospital. Bright purple and yellow crocuses pushed their way through the melting snow, and a huge flock of Canada geese honked a welcome from the beaver pond. Saskatoon and Knick-knick whinnied as Dave and Tory helped Adam from the car and into the lodge. Tory had to practically fight Kodiak and Sardidi away, they were so excited to see their master.

"It's all right, guys," Adam chuckled, reaching out to let the dogs lick his hand. "I'll be up and around in no time to take you for a hike."

Julia had prepared a recliner for Adam in front of the picture window in the living room where he had a bird's eye view of the valley and could see the animals as they passed by. She placed a little table beside it for his reading material and personal supplies.

Adam laughed when he saw the chair. "You guys had better be careful. I'm going to be so spoiled I'll be impossible to live with when I'm well," he said, sinking down into the comfortable chair. He leaned his head back and closed his eyes, sighing with pleasure. "Oh, but it feels good to be home."

A robin landed on the windowsill just outside and peered in at Adam. Throwing its head back, the bird began to sing at the top of its voice. Then it hopped up and down the sill, peeking in every few moments to look at Adam.

All day long, the bird kept up its vigil, leaving the window only to find food, then returning to continue its concert for the injured man.

"Why is this bird doing this?" Tory exclaimed, watching the robin in amazement. "I've never seen such a thing in all my life."

For a full week, the robin stayed on the window ledge. Then, as if on cue, the robin left, and a tiny Oregon junco took its place. With its jet-black hood, brown back, and pink sides and flanks, the little bird looked like a colorful painting out of a Roger Tory Peterson field guide. The junco flew to each window, fluttering in mid-air, then flew back down onto the windowsill directly in front of Adam's chair. He opened his little beak and let out a series of trills and chirps as if auditioning for an opera.

Two weeks passed and Adam gained strength every day. Tory prepared him many of his favorite dishes, tempting him with food she learned to make in Honduras. Gradually, the thin, sunken look disappeared from his face and his body slowly filled out so that he looked like himself again. The tiny junco stayed on the window ledge as long as Adam's weakness kept him in his chair. As soon as he felt strong enough to move around more, the little bird flew away, never to return.

"He was God's little emissary to me," Adam told Tory the third day after the bird disappeared. "He won't be back. His job was to keep me company for as long as I had to sit in that chair. And his work is done."

One morning in early April, Tory and Julia prepared a sumptuous breakfast of fresh buttermilk pancakes and thick, rich saskatoon syrup. The air outside felt so warm that Julia opened the double doors to the deck and let the sun's rays shine in, bathing the dining table in soft, warm light. Tory could see it shimmering on the dewdrops that clung to each stalk of dead grass in the valley, creating a rainbow effect. A herd of deer grazed near the tree line on the opposite side of the valley, jerking their heads up every few seconds to watch for Kodiak and Sardidi.

"I think I want to walk outside today," Adam announced as he swiped the last trace of the purple syrup from his plate with a forkful of pancake. He grinned at Tory. "Will you accompany me, m'lady?"

"Sure," Tory answered. She glanced at the table full of dishes to be cleared.

As if reading her thoughts, Julia picked up one of the dishes and said, "Go on, Tory. We'll get these. You take a walk with Adam." Dave nodded his agreement.

Kodiak and Sardidi bounded around Adam, ecstatic to see him outside again. He knelt down and wrapped his arms around their necks, burying his face in their coats. "I'm glad to see you guys, too," he said, his voice husky with emotion.

He stood up and headed for the corral, pulling a handful of wizened apple slices from his jeans' pocket. "Here you go, Sas. Here, Knick," he called. The Belgians thundered over to the gate, nickering a welcome. He held the apple pieces out, smiling as Saskatoon pinned his ears flat against his head and chased Knick-knick away before taking his share of the apple.

"Some things never change," Adam said, chuckling. He turned to Tory, his face suddenly sober. "There's something else that hasn't changed. I want to talk with you about it."

Tory watched the sunlight play on Adam's handsome face, soaking up the pure pleasure of just being with him, knowing that he was going to be OK.

I know I'll never view Adam the same, Father, she thought as she looked up at him. *I'll treasure every moment I have with him for just what it is: a pure gift from You. Thank You for giving him back to me.*

"What is it?" she asked, reaching up and gently brushing a stray lock of unruly dark hair from his forehead.

Adam reached out and pulled Tory close to him. She could feel the thumping of his heart as he held her. "I got a phone call from a friend of mine in Oregon," he said. "He told me about a Christian counseling training center in Portland called Good Samaritan Ministries. I want to go. I want to get the education I need to start our own retreat center like Border Mountain. Will you go?"

Tory lifted her head from Adam's chest and looked around her. Tiny green leaves like kitten's ears sprouted from the silvery branches of the aspen trees. A flock of mallards quacked noisy greetings to each other as they flew in for a landing on the beaver pond. Saskatoon pushed his nose into the small of her back, knocking her off balance.

"You scamp," she scolded, turning to face him. She ran her fingers through his thick, creamy mane. "I can't imagine leaving you. Or you." She reached out and touched Knick-knick's soft muzzle. Then she turned and looked into Adam's blue eyes.

"I *will* go," she said softly. "I've known for awhile that God was going to send us away from here. I know He has something for us and I'm with you. All the way."

Adam buried his face in her hair and sighed deeply. "Good," he said. "I was counting on it."

Somewhere in the distance a mountain lion screamed, but Tory felt no fear. Somehow the wilderness held no threat to her now. *I've seen the worst it can offer, Father,* she thought. *And none of it has been able to take us out of Your hand. I know we can trust You for every challenge the future has to offer, too.*

She slipped her hand into Adam's, and together they walked back inside.

TEN TIPS ON FEEDING YOUR HORSE

1. Feed regularly, the same time each day. If working your horse, feed him twice a day, but never just before or after a workout.

2. Keep the doors to your feed room locked. Horses can easily founder from overeating.

3. If it becomes necessary to alter your feeding schedule, do it gradually over a period of days to allow your horse's digestive system to adjust.

4. Do not feed grain or hay that has become moldy or spoiled. It can make your horse sick.

5. Avoid feeding dusty hay.

6. If your horse spills his feed when he eats, feed him in a smaller pan inside a large one so the feed doesn't spill on the ground and get dirty.

7. Provide plenty of fresh, clean water. Make it available continuously. If you're on a pack trip or at a show, be sure to water your horse two or three times a day.

8. Keep a mineral block available to your horse at all times.

9. Adjust the amount of grain you feed your horse according to his condition and alertness.

10. For a horse who is doing light work, feed approximately ½ pound grain and 1½ pounds hay for every 100 lbs. of body weight. (1 lb. grain = 1 qt.; a bale of hay usually weighs about 45-50 lbs.)

Safety Do's and Don'ts

1. *Do* approach, saddle, and mount a horse from his left side. (This tradition dates back to the days when knights carried big swords on their left sides and found out that it was easier to throw their right leg over the saddle.)

2. *Don't* walk up behind a horse without warning him that you are there. Speak to him as you approach. Horses can't see what is immediately behind them, and they instinctively kick to protect this blind spot.

3. *Do* keep your voice quiet and your touch calm. Shouting or beating an excited horse only makes him more upset. He needs to sense your confidence to be able to calm down.

4. *Don't* wrap reins, lead ropes, or saddle strings around your hands, wrists, or body. Even the gentlest of horses may spook.

5. *Do* walk beside your horse (not in front of him) when leading him. Hold his lead rope near the halter or his reins near the bit.

6. *Don't* tie your horse using the bridle reins. Fasten a strong lead rope to his halter and tie him high (level of his back or higher) and close to a post or tree (something solid). Make sure there's not enough slack in the rope for him to get a leg over and tangle himself up.

7. *Do* slow your horse to a walk when crossing pavement, bridges, ice, or any surface on which your

horse could lose his footing.

8. *Don't* mount your horse in a barn or near a fence. This will protect you from the possibility of a cracked head or cut leg.

9. *Do* check all straps before riding to make sure they are in good condition (girth, cinch, curb, reins).

10. *Don't* tease your horse or let him nibble at you. These habits lead to biting and other bad habits.

Horse Body Language

Ears

Turned back, but in a relaxed position: Listening to what's behind him.

Turned forward, in relaxed position: Interested in what's in front of him.

Pointed both right and left at the same time, relaxed: Listening to what's happening on both sides.

Straight forward and stiff: Nervous and excited. Alert for danger ahead.

Pointed stiffly back: Nervous about what's going on behind him. May kick, because he can't see what's happening in his blind spot.

Flat against head: Very angry. May bite or kick. Aggressive.

Droopy: Sleepy, resting, calm.

Tail

Tucked down tightly: Horse is sensing danger to his rear end. He may kick, buck, or bolt.

Switching tail back and forth: Irritated. It may be at something the rider is doing that tickles or annoys him, or it may be at a fly that's biting him.

Held high and arched: Proud, stimulated, enjoying himself.

Hoof Care

- Have hooves trimmed by a farrier about once every six weeks.
- If your horse is running in the pasture or on soft roads only, you may not need to have metal shoes put on his feet, but if you're riding him in rocky areas or on pavement, he should have his feet protected with shoes.
- Keep your horse's stall clean and dry.
- Before and after riding, clean the hoof with a pick, working from heel to toe, carefully removing rocks and mud around the frog.

Care of Tack

- Clean leather equipment after each use.
- Use glycerin saddle soap to clean.
- Applying a treatment of linseed oil at least once a month or so will protect the leather and keep it supple, preventing cracking.
- Store leather equipment in a dry place.
- If equipment gets wet, store it at room temperature to dry. Never dry leather with heat.
- Store your saddle on a saddle rack to help protect its structure. Twist the stirrups out and run a broom handle through them while being stored.

BIBLE TRUTHS "CHEAT SHEET"

With *A Horse Called Saskatoon,* JoAnne Nowack's series of books for teens ends. The author has included in the story line of these five books information on the care and training of horses that will enable the reader to earn the Pathfinder horsemanship honor.

Nowack has also woven throughout the story line the 27 Fundamental Beliefs (in some form). She has put together this "cheat sheet" that lists which beliefs can be found in which book. It is the publisher's hope that this topical index will be a helpful resource.